Signed by the authors

The ofline diary's

THE OFFLINE DIARIES

Yomi Adegoke & Elizabeth Uviebinené

THE OFFLINE DIARIES

AS TOLD BY

ADE AND SHANIC

HarperCollins Children's Books

Illustrated by
equitia Andrews
Ruthine Burton

First published in the United Kingdom by
HarperCollins *Children's Books* in 2022
HarperCollins *Children's Books* is a division of HarperCollins*Publishers* Ltd
1 London Bridge Street
London SE1 9GF

www.harpercollins.co.uk

HarperCollins*Publishers*
1st Floor, Watermarque Building, Ringsend Road
Dublin 4, Ireland

1

HB ISBN 978–0–00–844477–8
SPECIAL EDITION ISBN 978–0–00–855335–7
TPB ISBN 978–0–00–844478–5

Yomi Adegoke, Elizabeth Uviebinené, Tequitia Andrews and Ruthine Burton
assert the moral right to be identified as the authors and illustrators of the work respectively.

A CIP catalogue record for this title is available from the British Library.

Typeset in Zemke Hand ITC 12/19pt, Alcoholica 14/19pt and
Agenda 11/16pt by Sorrel Packham
Printed and bound in the UK using 100% renewable electricity at CPI Group (UK) Ltd

MIX
Paper from
responsible sources
FSC™ C007454

This book is produced from independently certified FSC™ paper
to ensure responsible forest management.

For more information visit: www.harpercollins.co.uk/green

For best friends everywhere
E. U.

For the younger Yomi and Elizabeth —
we couldn't have done it without you
Y. A.

Chapter 1

Ade

Dear Diary,

I DON'T KNOW WHY I BOTHER. I can barely hear myself think these days, even when locked away in my room. I've turned off the telly, kicked Funmi into Bisi's new room (all three of us will fight about that later, but she's out so I'm enjoying the quiet before the storm), shut the curtains, put a pillow up against the door and still — non-stop racket. Aunty Kim says my writing is important, and especially so now because, even with all the drama, I still manage to write down what I think and feel and stuff. Sometimes I agree with her, but other times I'm just like, what's the point of trying when no one

1

ever shuts up around here?

You know what makes it even more annoying? The fact that I'm the one constantly getting told off for making too much noise, and for having too much attitude. By my mum, by my old teachers, probably by my new ones when I start school on Monday. Any time I say what I think, it's, 'Ade, you're being disrespectful,' or, 'Ade, you're being rude.'

That's why I write so much — when I try to say how I feel in real life, at home or at my old school, I'm told I'm 'talking back'. It's like, if someone is older than you, they're allowed to talk at you, not to you. If you disagree with them, you shouldn't respond, as they'll say that's rude too! Having any sort of opinion on an issue is an issue.

> But I'm gonna say what I think anyway – even if it's just in this diary.

At least when I'm a famous novelist, and I eventually publish this, it will be evidence of how crazy my family is. This place is a madhouse – Funmi is so hyper and so randomly demanding I don't call her my 'little sister' any more because, as she claims, 'I'm not little – we're the same height.' No wonder Bisi is always having a go at Funmi – she bounces around the house like an idiot ball and usually ends up in Bisi's new room, knocking something expensive over in the process. Then Bisi shouts at her, Funmi cries and Bisi gets shouted at by Mum and, instead of crying, Bisi gets angry (or angrier) and goes back to ignoring us all.

Bisi has a go at everyone though, to be fair; sixteen going on sixty, she's a total killjoy and a terrible advert for getting older. She is always skulking around the old house, in a mood about coursework or spots or another stupid boyfriend gone wrong (which she isn't even allowed to have — sometimes, when she used to sneak out to see whoever it was, she'd pay me in chocolate for my silence). Bisi can and will argue with anyone. Once, when we were out shopping with Mum, I saw her square up to a mannequin she thought had bumped into her!

Note to self: when I grow up, skip the spotty, moany, sulky bit and get right to the glamorous bestselling-author bit.

And then there's Mum. If she isn't complaining about the dishes that have only just hit the sink, she's pestering me about homework I don't even have. Meanwhile, *he* is asking me why I seem to talk non-stop to everyone but *him*.

Duh — 'Because you're annoying and I don't like you! Well, I like you even less than everyone else, which is saying something.'

And then Mum starts up again about how I have to be nice to *him* because *he's* my stepdad, and I remind her *he* was *her* choice, not ours. Plus, it's all *his* fault we had to move house in the first place. And then Bisi and Funmi pipe up that they quite like *him* actually, and I remind them that not everyone can be so easily bought off with Alton Towers trips and H&M vouchers.

I swear, if my sisters didn't look pretty much exactly like me — same slanty brown eyes and long, lanky limbs — I would think I was adopted. I'm the second youngest in this house (I'm just about to turn thirteen finally!), but half the time I feel like the only one with any sense. They all gang up on me — even Funmi takes Bisi and Mum's side when it comes to *him*, although she's only been my little sister for, oh, seven years, and known *him* all of ten minutes. What makes it even worse is that *he* will be the one sticking up for me (the suck-up), trying to make me look bad by playing the saint. Whatever. We'll only go and have the same fight again in a few days. Same old poo, different toilet.

Well, different poo and different toilet now, since we're in this horrible new house, in this horrible new town, and I'm about to start some horrible new school. We've been here a week already and it still feels all wrong — and, to make the worst of matters even WORSE, we're only here because *he* got a new job, which means we've had to leave everything behind just so *he* can be closer to it. And that means I'm further away from everything that matters to me: my school. My friends. My favourite park. The old house. Aunty Kim. Dad. The local park here is a good thirty-minute walk away and the closest shopping centre is a whole bus journey! Mum thinks the fact my room is bigger makes up for it, but I still have to share it with Funmi, and she's still a pain, so nothing's really changed except that things have got even more annoying.

Today, though, there was the teeniest, tiniest of signs that maybe this place isn't a total dump. Even in this new town, I can't escape Mum's endless visits to the hairdresser's. She dragged me and Funmi along to get her hair braided yet again (she's going for a copper colour this time, and, despite what she thinks, it doesn't make her look any younger).

She was recommended this place on the high street called Powers. It looked pretty dingy from the outside and even had one window blacked out with a bin liner. But, when we got inside, it was much nicer than the usual salons Mum goes to — it smelled like vanilla and shea butter, and was shiny and sleek, like a laboratory. There were two women in black aprons with *Powers* sewn on, in silver italics, like the sign outside; one was lathering up a customer's hair with

soapy

lavender

bubbles

and another younger stylist was texting away on her phone lazily as she waited for something to do.

'Hello, ladies!' a booming voice greeted us from behind the counter. 'How can I help you today?'

It was the salon owner — Matthew — and he was tall and slim with a serious face. After showing him a picture of what she wanted, he took Mum over to one of the stylists, and she sat down wearily, prepping herself for four hours of haircare.

At this point, I was already dreading the thought of spending the whole afternoon flicking through magazines older than I am and dodging the bogeys Funmi was flicking at me (yes, she still picks her nose — so childish). I began rummaging through my bag, so I could spend a bit of time writing in my diary, and then Matthew turned to me. He glanced at the diary and grinned.

'You must be around my daughter's age,' he said with a nod. 'Let me introduce you to her — I have a feeling you two will get on.'

She was sitting on a brown leather couch in the corner, and had these really cool chunky braids that stopped just below her chin. She was also scribbling in a big pink diary — a big pink diary that looked exactly like MINE! Same colour, same design, only hers wasn't decorated with all my fab stickers and cutouts.

'This is Shanice,' Matthew said, gesturing at his daughter. She looked up, seemed to size me up and went back to writing vigorously. 'Shanice, this is . . .'

'I'm Ade,' I said, shuffling on the spot. 'New to the area.'

'Nice to meet you,' Shanice said, glancing up after a moment. 'And nice journal!' We both began to grin.

Here comes the really cool part: since we've moved here, I don't think I've had a real conversation with anyone I don't already know, but Shanice and I spoke non-stop at the salon. She loves writing — like me! Her favourite colour is pink too. We don't agree on everything, and that's fine —

she hates PE and isn't a fan of salt-and-vinegar crisps (nobody's perfect, I guess).

We were interrupted every so often by Funmi doing something gross, but guess what? Shanice just laughed it off every time! Even the non-stop farting! It wasn't even embarrassing. But, most importantly, she has a diary too, though she calls hers a journal, which sounds so mature and posh.

I said I'd give hers a makeover — sequins, stickers, glitter, photos, the lot. I have NEVER told any of my schoolfriends about my diary because I assumed they'd think it was a bit babyish. But Shanice says it's actually very grown-up and a good way of dealing with your thoughts and feelings and stuff. She's really nice and the one good thing so far about this move.

We got on so well that, by the time Mum's hair was finished, it felt like no time had passed at all. And Mum was really happy that I'd made a friend (though it's, like, chill out, Mum — I've barely known her a day, ugh). Anyway, we're going to stay in touch and hopefully hang out soon. Today was different, and I think Shanice is a bit different too. Just sent her an invite on ChatBack. Let's see if she accepts . . .

Chapter 2
Shanice

Hey,

It felt weird when Mrs P gave me this as a present on my birthday. A whole book to write stuff in. (Mrs P is a teacher at Archbishop Academy – one of the nicest in the school – and she also happens to live on our street, and used to babysit me sometimes when I was little.)

'Happy birthday, Shanice,' she said. 'Here, this is your very own special journal – I want you to write about anything and everything in it.'

Okay. What's a journal? I thought to myself, and

what trick is Mrs P trying to pull? She could tell I was confused.

'Isn't this a diary?' I said.

She looked at me with a cheeky smile like she knew a secret I didn't. 'Shanice Powers, you're brimming with ideas and creativity. You need somewhere to write them all down – no more scraps of paper. Some day, one of your ideas will change the world.'

Now it was my turn to look at her in a weird way.

Sure. Change the world? Isn't that what politicians do? It sounds *sooo* long and boring. But I guessed it was about time I graduated from scraps of paper and on to a journal. Dad says if he sees one more bit of paper in my room he's going to flush them all down the toilet. Gosh, he can be so dramatic. He basically went ballistic last week when he found that I'd written on a 'very important letter' – he wouldn't shut up about it all afternoon. How was I meant to know? If it was that important, then it shouldn't have been left on the kitchen table. Duh.

I'd had an idea at breakfast, and so of course I had to write it down quickly somewhere. Maybe on his 'very important letter' wasn't such a great idea. But anyway I always have ideas when eating Coco Pops. I'm only allowed them once a week. **(My dentist says I'm addicted to sugar. Who isnt???)**

So this journal is the first time I'm writing stuff down all in one place. Hmmm. My head gets so full of random muddled thoughts, and I just have to get them out!!! I need to remember to carry the journal with me everywhere too. At the age of seven, I got into so much trouble when I was caught writing on walls. I saw Dad doing it first: 'Come, child, stand up straight and let me measure you,' he'd say, and then he'd mark my height on the wall with a pencil.

Dad thinks the journal is a good idea, seeing as, 'You don't talk to anybody these days.'

I think he sometimes wishes I was more outgoing and chatty. I overheard him on the phone to someone (I suspect Mrs P), and he called me a loner. The thing is, I just never know what to say any more, to anyone . . . ever since Mum . . .

I just don't understand why Dad is on my case so much. At least my bedroom doesn't have smelly socks and empty crisp packets like my older brother James's

13

room. When he stays locked up in there, Dad doesn't say anything, but if I do – it's a problem. James thinks the world revolves round him – and it does! I'm sick of being treated differently.

But anyway today was another Saturday sitting in Dad's shop, which is always boring, but at least I could journal. It was either that or go to Mrs P's house. I know she means well, but I find her suffocating at times. Plus, her dog Rufus doesn't like me and barks too much. Maybe Dad's right and I am a loner.

I know my next birthday is going to be a weird one. I do want to be alone. I miss our birthday trips to the ice-cream parlour, when Dad would get me waffles with extra cream and sprinkles on top, then Mum would get fake annoyed and say, 'That's your lot, missy. This is all the sugar you're getting until your next birthday.'

Of course it never was. I used to have her wrapped round my little finger.

Dad got me clothes this year. How boring! Who wants a T-shirt with *Little Miss Misunderstood* and a silver elephant on it? What am I – five? He thought it was funny too! I think I might put it in a bin when he's not looking. The only good thing about it is that it's pink – at least he got that right. Can you imagine walking around with a T-shirt saying *Little Miss Misunderstood*? Yeah, great way to make myself even more of a target at school than I already am.

At least at the shop I can people-watch. I love observing the customers and then making up stories about them.

This Saturday, a woman comes in with a big brown fur coat, black knee-high boots and a huge floppy hat. She looks like a spy, as if she's hiding something. I haven't seen her in here before, probably a newbie – she seems unsure of her surroundings. I see her whispering something to Dad, and he raises his hand to his mouth and gasps, as if they're having a secret conversation. What did I say about my dad being dramatic? I can tell he's trying not to laugh. I wonder what's going on there. Why do people take hair so seriously? It's just hair.

If people aren't having secret convos in here, they're being really loud and complaining. Adults are weird. Do any of them actually like each other? Today Janet, one of my dad's regulars, is moaning about her husband: 'He never puts anything away. It's like living with another child,' she says from under the dryer.

They never think I'm listening in – I'm invisible in the shop, and that's how I like it.

Just as I was starting to get *really* hungry, Dad walked over with a girl I'd never seen before. She introduced herself as Ade. She reminded me of one of those cool girls at school, with her hair braided up in a bun and a butterfly clip on each side.

She spotted my journal, and her eyes lit up. 'Is that your diary?' she asked excitedly.

It turned out that Ade has a diary too, and wanted to know why I call mine a journal. I told her they're the same thing – basically for writing stuff down in. She asked why it didn't have sequins and stickers on it – Ade is really girly. I wouldn't mind a sticker or two, but sequins are a bit much.

Ade seemed very confident and outgoing, maybe a little too outgoing. I told her I got my journal as a birthday present, then she started asking me a million questions about things like star signs. Mum used to be into all that stuff. I remember her telling me I was a Virgo. Ade got really excited about that: apparently, it means we're going to get on. We chatted loads, and she told me she had just moved to the area – not sure why anyone would want to move here. Nothing interesting happens in this place . . . ever. Our conversation was probably the most exciting thing that had happened to me in ages. Her sister Funmi is hilarious too. What a family.

I got so hungry that my belly growled, and Ade unzipped her pink backpack and offered me a packet of salt-and-vinegar crisps. First of all, who actually chooses to eat salt-and-vinegar crisps? And, second of all, she's so nice!!! I never make friends this easily. Okay, not gonna get my hopes up just yet – it's been one conversation. I probably won't see her much anyway. Ohhhhh, she's just sent me a friend invite on ChatBack . . .

CHAPTER 3

∎

CHATBACK

@PrincessSuperAde: Hey! Nice meeting you today :)

@_Shannyxo: Hey :) You too.
Made my day at the hair shop go much quicker!

@PrincessSuperAde: You made my day being dragged
along to the hair shop with my mum and sister go
much quicker too, so thanks :') lol.

@PrincessSuperAde: What are you going to be doing
for the rest of the weekend? Anything fun planned?

@_Shannyxo: I mean, unless being sat in the shop helping my dad out is considered fun then . . . nope :')
You?

@PrincessSuperAde: Me either. My mum is making us go to church with her tomorrow morning, first thing. We've only been here five minutes, not sure how she's managed to find one already . . .

@_Shannyxo: Loooool that was fast! You should definitely try and stop by the shop after if you have time. Would be really nice to chat again.
You can bring Funmi along too.

@PrincessSuperAde: I'll only come if Funmi is NOT allowed to!!!

@_Shannyxo: Okay, deal lol! But she's actually sweet!

@PrincessSuperAde: You say that because you don't know her properly yet lol.

@_Shannyxo: Looool. Well, she can't be as
bad as my brother.

@PrincessSuperAde: :') We'll see!

@_Shannyxo: When you do come next, you can
decorate my journal if you still want to.

@PrincessSuperAde: Really? Yay! With pink stuff, of
course ;) This is going to be so fun. Can't believe I've
actually managed to find something I like about this
town!

@_Shannyxo: Awww, thanks! I like you too!

@PrincessSuperAde: I do miss my old place though.
And my school. And my mates :(All the memories.

@_Shannyxo: That sucks :(Hopefully, you'll make
some new even better ones here though?

@PrincessSuperAde: Hopefully :)

@_Shannyxo::)

@_Shannyxo: Ugh, my dad's lost the remote and obviously it's up to me, never James, to help him find it >:(I'm going to go now, but speak to you soon?

@PrincessSuperAde: Yeah, cool :) Speak soon! We can sort out when we're meeting up next and stuff.

@_Shannyxo: Yeah, sure. I'll probably message you after school for a moan too. Another day in hell, i.e. Archbishop Academy.

@PrincessSuperAde: What :O??? You go to Archbishop Academy?

@_Shannyxo: Yeah, why, have you heard of it?

@PrincessSuperAde: Heard of it? I start on Monday :')

@_Shannyxo: NO WAY :O

@PrincessSuperAde: YES WAY!

@_Shannyxo: This is completely crazy!

@PrincessSuperAde: This is the best news EVER, is what it is! What tutor group are you in?

@_Shannyxo: I'm in 8O . . . how about you?
Please say you're in 8O . . .

@PrincessSuperAde: I'M IN 8O.

@_Shannyxo: Are you just saying that?

@PrincessSuperAde: Shanice, I'm in 8O! My tutor is called Mr Oppong???

@_Shannyxo: OMG. We're in the same tutor group!

@PrincessSuperAde: This just gets better and better.

@_Shannyxo: It does! Mr Oppong sucks, but at least you'll make the mornings a bit less rubbish!

@PrincessSuperAde: Yay! I can't believe I'm excited about school lol.

@_Shannyxo: :D

@_Shannyxo: So I guess I'll see you on Monday?

@PrincessSuperAde: I guess you will! Let's meet outside the school gates <3

Chapter 4

Shanice

Hey,

I woke up to the sound of my dad blasting out reggae this morning. He always says it reminds him of his childhood in St Lucia. 'You kids don't get it,' he says. I always loved its warm weather, clear blue sea and sandy beaches. So I do kind of get what he's saying! But I'll never tell him that!

He was really going for it today, playing all his favourites, which I've heard a million and ten times before. I think it just reminds him of Mum. He does this in the

mornings, when he misses her the most. It's his way
of remembering her. They met at university and
became inseparable. 'They were really in love,'
my aunties always say.

The last time we went to St Lucia was
probably one of my last happy memories
of us as a family. We almost missed our
flight because – surprise, surprise –
James couldn't get his act together.

He didn't know what to pack, so wanted to take everything and anything. If you saw the amount he did eventually pack, it was actually crazy – as if he thought he was a famous model being flown out to a Paris fashion show like in the movies. He had a massive row with Dad the morning we had to leave for the airport, which made us so late we almost missed our flight. Is it bad to say that I wished we *had* missed it so James would get the blame and the golden child would have been a little less golden?

One thing I would say about my big brother though is that he does have sick dress sense, and sometimes I catch myself admiring how well he puts outfits together and makes everything look effortless and (dare I say) cool. I can't believe I just wrote that. **He most definitely isn't cool to me, but to the untrained eye he might be.**

He gets his fashion sense from Mum. She was effortlessly stylish in the way she dressed, and when she walked into a room people would stare at her. Her signature look was her long, waist-length blonde braids. Sometimes she put beads in them, which made so much noise they drove Dad crazy! But, when we were out and people admired them, he'd tell everyone it was his favourite hairstyle – adults are so fake! Dad always says he loved Mum's fierceness and individuality. I agree with that. She was never afraid to be herself.

Anyway, that was a good trip to St Lucia. So, even though Dad wakes me up with this loud music, it really does make me feel warm and fuzzy inside. St Lucia is like a home away from home. Sometimes, when I'm feeling a bit meh, it's one of my favourite places to daydream about.

I tried to sit alone with my thoughts before I mustered the courage to go downstairs. I really love daydreaming. There's just something special about closing your eyes and imagining things. I can daydream so vividly, it almost feels real – I think it's my superpower!

I came down to find Dad trying to make breakfast, and when I say trying I really mean trying. He always insists on cooking breakfast every morning. He does this elaborate thing when he's frying an egg. It's like that egg is the most important thing in the world. He looks at it, sometimes even sings to it. It's as if he's trying to persuade the egg to taste really good! He does his best with the cooking, but it's always a bit bland these days.

What I really wanted to eat was my leftover birthday

cake. Seven centimetres of red-velvet goodness. Yeah, I'd much rather have that for breakfast.

I really can't believe Ade is going to be in my class. She's the girl I met yesterday at Dad's salon. She seems like good vibes and, trust me, that class needs hella good vibes.

I told Dad about Ade going to my school, and he's surprised that I actually like her because I don't like anyone . . . apparently. And he's really happy that she'll be in my class – and, to be honest, I'm super excited too. Finally, I might just have a reason to turn up to that dreaded place every day!

However, this Sunday is another long day at Dad's salon. I'd much rather just stay at home and do some writing, but I'm somehow not grown-up enough according to Dad. I'm old enough to help out in the shop though. Interesting how adults make up rules to suit themselves.

Anyway, I tried to avoid everyone in there today. Whenever the door opened, I couldn't help but hope it was Ade walking in. But it was only Dad's usual customers who come in on a Sunday after church. Always so dressed up and always so loud.

The kids at school used to make fun of me because

29

Dad does hair. They said it was a girly thing and not what dads should do. I came home once in tears because one of the Double-A girls – the meanest ones in my year – made a comment that really hurt my feelings. But I had to hold it in as I didn't want them to see that it bothered me. Deep down, I just wanted to burst out crying and yell back that they didn't know what they were talking about and to shut their big mouths. But I didn't – I sat in the girls' toilet all lunchtime, praying nobody would come in. Can you imagine eating lunch in the toilet? Very icky and not very nice.

But that's the thing about those girls: they're not nice. **When I ran home that day, Mum gave me the biggest hug and made me feel safe.** One of her favourite sayings was, 'Sticks and stones may break my bones, but words will never hurt me.' I did feel better once she warmed me up with one of her famous hot chocolates with marshmallows on the side, and we'd watched my favourite film. Anyway, who gets to decide what anyone should do when they grow up?

Mrs P asked me what I wanted to be once, and at first I didn't know how to answer.

'Er, I dunno. Maybe a vet?'

She looked at me in the way only Mrs P would. 'Interesting choice – I never did like pets when I was growing up, but cats are nice!'

Of all the animals, she chooses a cat – she's so dull! Honestly, I find cats super boring. They just sit there – not exciting enough for me! I love dogs, but they're still kind of basic. Once you've played with them a few times, there's not much else to do. My favourite animals are all the really exotic ones that you don't find in my local area – the ones you see on safari or on those TV shows that have nature's coolest-looking creatures. Like an African lion, which the voiceover always refers to as the 'king of the jungle' – although I'm not so sure how they rule the jungle as they always look very laid-back – and anyway do they even live in jungles? I'm fascinated by zebras; they have the most beautiful black-and-white striped coats. Dad says each individual's stripes are unique.

I would love to go on safari one day. I can't imagine anything more dreamy. Whenever I see them advertised on TV, I always rush to turn the volume up. James just doesn't get it. But I believe animals are better than

31

humans: they don't bother anyone; they're not mean for no reason; they just need food and water and that's it – they leave you alone.

Lucky for me, right opposite Dad's salon is a pet shop, Petsland. It wasn't open today, but it's my favourite place to sneak off to when he's not looking. The owner, Ms Davies, loves me off. She always starts every visit by telling me what the animals have been up to. She has the biggest of eyes, which light up when she's talking about her favourite pets. She lets me feed them if there's time, and sometimes she even allows me to help out with cleaning and stuff.

There's one bearded dragon that I just love and I've kind of adopted. Dad says that if I show him I can be responsible then one day he might allow me to permanently adopt it. How am I meant to show him what being responsible is??? **He says I need to clean my room more and lay the table, but what's that got to do with looking after a lizard? Like really.**

We were meant to get a dog, but guess who's allergic? James. When Mum and Dad were toying with the idea, we went to see a puppy, but all James could do was sneeze and sneeze the whole time we were there. At first, we thought he was playing around, but, after tests, the doctor said he was allergic. That put a stop to the puppy plans immediately. So annoying. I think that's when I started to go off James – how can you be allergic to a harmless little puppy? I think Mum and Dad were kind of annoyed too, though they never said anything.

So, yeah, I might just become a vet after all. James had to do work experience at Petsland last summer for two weeks, and all he did was complain. He said he couldn't imagine anything more 'boring, bland and soul-sucking'.

I just thought: *Well, that's not going to be me when I become a vet.* Ms Davies from Petsland has already confirmed I can do my work experience with her when the time comes.

Mrs P says I'll need to study hard if I'm to become a vet, urghhhh. Talking about studying, school is tomorrow. The only reason I'm not dreading it is because I'll get to see Ade again. I wonder what she'll make of everyone.

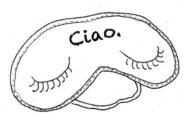

Chapter 5

Ade

Dear Diary,

I DON'T WANT TO SAY I KNOW EVERYTHING, BUT I KNOW EVERYTHING! As soon as I saw Shanice, I just got the feeling that I was in the right place at the right time and *BOOM*: next thing you know, it turns out we're in the same year at the same school? It's mad! But amazing!

I usually take ages to get up in the morning for school, but I was awake before the alarm today. I wasn't that excited about school, as I was *not* looking forward to being the new girl, but was definitely excited to see Shanice again.

My new uniform is okay, I guess, not as nice as the

one from my old school. There's a bright red jumper and a black blazer with the same red on the lapels and the school crest in the corner, and a black-and-red tie. I've seen worse.

Since it was my first day, I decided to make a bit of an impression. I borrowed a pair of Bisi's earrings — the blue sparkly hoops — to match my blue hair clips. I spritzed a bit of her perfume on my neck and wrists for good measure too; I hope she doesn't notice this time. I swear she measures the bottle with a ruler; she always knows when I've used a bit, but this time I was one step ahead and added a bit of water to top the bottle up. I even nearly managed to convince Mum to let me take the bus, rather than her giving me a lift (I wanted to make the right impression on my first day — new school, new me and all that), but we agreed that she would drop me off round the corner, which was a touch less embarrassing. Can't have it all, I suppose . . .

Mum is so happy that I'm walking in on the first

day with a friend. She wouldn't stop smiling over breakfast (a bowl of that wholegrain cereal Bisi insists on instead of Coco Pops, which she says is healthier, bleurgh).

'See how God works!' Mum kept saying. 'It was fate, me getting my braids done that day, and, if you hadn't come with me, you wouldn't have met Shanice!'

'Shanice! Shanice!' Funmi said, spilling orange juice all over the table with excitement. 'When can we play with her again, Ade? She was so fun!'

I hadn't realised she'd been listening to the conversation – she had one arm in the cereal box, trying to fish out a free toy that wasn't there.

'I'm seeing her today, remember?' I reminded her. 'We're going to the same school!'

'Not fair!' she shouted. 'How come you get to play with her? Can I go too?'

'No babies allowed at Archbishop,' I said, sticking my tongue out. 'We're going to have loads of fun without you.'

Funmi made a kind of hiccuping noise, the one she always does before she pretends to cry. 'Not . . .

fair . . . Mummy!' she said, stamping her foot.

'Well, I think it's amazing you've made a new friend before starting, Ade,' he said, trying to insert himself into the conversation. 'That's half the worry when you're new, isn't it?' I ignored him; even *he* couldn't ruin the start to my first day at Archbishop Academy.

It's much bigger than my old school and is up a massively, massively steep road. As soon as I realised this, I regretted getting Mum to drop me off that far away — the walk was so tiring! The school's surrounded by loads of fields and woods and stuff too. The thing about this new town is it takes ages to get from one place to another.

When I finally made it to the entrance, Shanice was waiting for me by the school gates, as we'd agreed. I spotted her immediately among the sea of people because of her chunky braids and jumper. Though she was in the same uniform as everyone else, she looked different, somehow more casual. Everything seemed a bit too big on her — her jumper sagged and was more burgundy than bus red like ours. Her trousers were baggy and her shoes slightly slipped off at the back. I'd forgotten how short she was!

'Hey!' she said. 'Nice earrings!'

'Thanks. They're Bisi's. I'd tell her you like them, but she doesn't know I've got them!'

She giggled, and we chatted about the rest of our weekend as we made our way into the classroom. The classrooms in Archbishop Academy seemed bigger than in my old school, with rows of grey chairs and blue lockers at the back, and the pupils in 8O were all sitting around, chatting, before the bell went.

'I can't wait to tell you all about everyone here,' said Shanice. 'There's so much to say.'

That's when I heard Mr Oppong, our tutor, clear his throat behind us.

'Here we go,' Shanice said under her breath.

'Shanice, I see you've already met your new classmate, Ade,' he said.

Shanice looked even shorter standing next to Mr Oppong, who is easily seven feet tall. ('He never fails to remind us how he nearly went pro as a basketball player till his "injury", Shanice told me later, shaking her head. 'Well, now you're stuck teaching us PE, mate!')

'Yeah, I have. We met at my dad's shop over the weekend. Can't wait to tell her all about the school,' she said with a hint of sarcasm.

Mr Oppong cleared his throat again and turned to me. 'Yes, well. Welcome to Archbishop Academy and to 8O, Ade. We're thrilled you'll be joining us.'

'Thanks, sir. I'm very happy to be here,' I lied.

'And, since the pair of you already seem to be firm friends, it would be nice if you could show Ade around the school and help her out on her first day,' he said to Shanice. 'Welcome her the Archbishop Academy way?'

'Yes, sir,' Shanice said.

'So with a lukewarm lunch of turkey slices and day-old gravy, and a locker that doesn't shut, sir?'

she said once we were out of earshot. I snorted.

Mr Oppong turned round and gave a tight smile. 'Please just make sure she's looked after.'

'Of course!' we both said.

'There you have it,' said Shanice. 'My least

39

favourite teacher at Archbishop. And that's saying something!'

'He seems all right to me!' I said. He came across as pretty laid-back.

'You wait and see,' she said. 'Remember I've been here a whole year already. He's the worst. But I can't wait for you to meet Mrs P!'

After the register, Shanice showed me around 8O: where my new locker would be, where I'd sit during registration. Then she turned her attention to the other pupils, pointing out the who's who of the class. She ran me through the names of most of the students, and I forgot all of them almost immediately — most of their faces too!

But two girls came in after registration, and they were very hard to miss. They both looked like they were in Year 10 at least. Their hair was worn in the same messy bun on top of their head, but one was blonde and the other had jet-black hair. Both were wearing black trainers — you're not allowed to wear trainers at Archbishop — and I could have sworn they both had light make-up on too, which is definitely banned. We had to be in for registration at

8.30 and first period was at 8.50 — they'd arrived at 8.49, and looked very chilled out about it.

'Good morning, girls,' Mr Oppong said, barely hiding his annoyance. 'Glad you could join us. We have a new pupil in our class — her name's Ade, and she's already been introduced to the rest of 8O, but since you were late—'

'Hey, Ade, nice to meet you!' The blonde cut him off in mid-moan. She wasn't even looking in my direction, and the other one didn't even bother to fake a smile. Then the bell went, and they legged it before he could properly have a go at them.

'Who are they?' I whispered to Shanice, kind of in awe. She rolled her eyes.

'Amy Parker and Aaliyah Saleem AKA Double A. Hands down the most popular girls in the school and hands down the meanest.

Two words: stay away. They'll eat you up and spit you back out when they've finished with you.'

'I take it you guys don't get along?' I asked.

'Definitely not. All they care about is clothes and

how many followers they can get on ChatBack. Not only are they super mean, but they're stupid too. It's, like, pick one bad thing to be!'

I laughed. 'Thanks for the heads-up. But, to be honest, they don't look like they're in the market for new friends anyway!' I said.

'Yep.' Shanice nodded. 'If your name doesn't begin with A, and you're not rude, obnoxious and ChatBack-obsessed, they aren't interested. You're only a third of the way there!'

I laughed again as the bell rang, and made my way to my first lesson of the day, maths with Mr Brockett and then physics with Mrs Buchanan. On the way out, the Double A with black hair said something as she passed me. 'Your earrings. Unreal!'

I looked at Shanice, who was as surprised as I was. The girl was out the door before I could even say thank you.

Both lessons were pretty boring, so it was great to be able to see Shanice again properly at lunch. I noticed that, although she had a few friends here and there, she was pretty quiet at Archbishop, definitely a bit of a loner who did her own thing.

After lunch, I had English with Mrs Adams and the famous Mrs P, the teaching assistant – Shanice and I share that class together, but sit separately because of the alphabetical seating plan.

The Double As (or 'double trouble' as I think they'd be better named) whispered all the way through the lesson, and the teacher didn't even notice!

I have to say I was disappointed in Shanice's favourite teacher, Mrs P. She's got greyish, mousy brown hair and squinty eyes that are always searching for trouble. And, like most teachers, she's pretty frumpy, with her cardigan and thick beige tights.

While I think I caught the attention of the Double As with my earrings, they also came to the attention of Mrs P. She confiscated them during the lesson. I have no idea why Shanice loves her so much.

'You just caught her on a bad day,' Shanice said.

I'm just hoping Bisi doesn't notice that the earrings are gone or I'm dead. But, all in all, it was a pretty good first day. I don't want to speak too soon, but think I'm going to like it here.

Chapter 6
Shanice

Hey!

School again today. The beginning of the school year is always a drag. I've noticed that parents do that very annoying thing of acting as if it's a fresh new start, when in fact it's just more of the same. Same school, same students and same annoying teachers. Back-to-school socks, back-to-school jumpers with all the promotions on the high street shouting at you as you walk past. Well, I don't want to get

BACK TO SCHOOL.

The only good thing about a new term is new stationery! It's the one part I do look forward to when starting a new school year. Dad didn't have time to take me stationery shopping, so I did it all online this time. He gave me a budget to get all my bits and bobs with. Fine by me – I knew what I wanted anyway.

I bought my usual notebooks, special paper for art class and boring maths stuff we were told to get. But what I really wanted were these pens that look proper grown-up. They're kind of old school, and they're called fountain pens. I bought them in a few colours; my favourites are the pink and purple, of course. I'm using the purple one now – it's so cool to write with, and I love using it for poems and stories in English. It came with this fancy metallic case that changes colour depending on how the light hits it. Sometimes it's a blue tint; other times it's purple.

Last year, I wanted to be home-schooled so badly. I begged Mum and Dad for ages and ages – I spent a whole day crying and pleading.

'Please, please, please, I'll do anything.'

'I'll be responsible.'

'I'll even clean James's room, like, every day.'

But they weren't having it.

'You get to start with a clean slate, new teachers, new friends, new experiences,' Mum told me.

Dad and Mum said that school was much tougher when they were my age, and that I don't know how easy I have it now. Just because we're not using those old computers and having to write on dusty chalkboards doesn't mean we do. If I never hear another 'in my day' lecture from Dad again, it'll be too soon.

They wouldn't last a minute at Archbishop Academy. They don't understand what it's like at this school. It's all about who's who, and if you're deemed a nobody on day one then you'll be a nobody for the rest of your time here.

So I didn't want to start at Archbishop Academy. I don't like change. And going to this school would be a massive upheaval I was not prepared for. I was very happy with the way things were at my primary school. I had friends there – it took me a while to make them, but in the end I enjoyed it.

'New faces, new places and new challenges can open up a whole new world for you, Shanice. You can't control everything – that's not how life works,' Mum said the night before my first day.

Rather than think of all the ways it could go wrong, I should picture myself having a good time instead, she said, calling it 'positive visualisation'. At first, I was very unsure – another thing adults say just to make you feel better, I thought suspiciously. She asked me to close my eyes and think of all the good outcomes rather than the bad ones. She said that would always be the best way to face my fears, because in life there will always be fears – it's how we deal with them that is the important thing.

'If you want a situation to go well, you have to feel it, think it and see it in your mind. If you think pessimistically about it, then all you have is just a ball of negativity, and that's no fun, now is it?'

We started off by closing our eyes and taking deep breaths, and then she asked me to visualise my perfect day at school. From my perfect breakfast to my perfect lesson. I did this for a few minutes and sneakily glanced at her. **With her eyes closed, and the sun hitting her face, her long eyelashes curled so tightly and a half-smile on her face, she looked beautiful. Like an angel.**

When I do try to positively visualise good outcomes, it does make me feel better. And, now that I know Mum is

up there like a real-life angel, watching me, my bellyful
of butterflies turns into a warm, happy feeling. I guess
that's our thing, the way we communicate with each
other.

I didn't win the home-schooling battle – surprise, surprise.

The last thing I was expecting on my first day was a
school buddy. Every new starter at Archbishop Academy
is given one. It's meant to give newbies a chance to
bond with older kids, who are supposed to be our
'positive role models and mentors' in school. Someone
to help and support us at break times, as we settle into
school life.

We were meant to ask them questions about our new
school and tell them any worries we had. I overheard
one of the boys in my class ask if it was true that older
students push Year 7s' heads down the toilets, and
another girl wanted to know if you had to dissect pigs'
eyes in science.

I really didn't want to ask any silly questions like that.
My buddy was a girl called Sophie. And she was not
what I was expecting at all. Sophie was really popular –

probably the most popular girl in Year 8. She had an air about her – everyone wanted to be her friend. She was confident and very pretty.

I wondered why they paired me up with her. Why was she *my* buddy?

'I'm here to help you handle some experiences I've been through.' She took a deep breath like she had a prepared speech ready.

She was one of those people that chewed gum really loudly and spoke really quickly. She looked me straight in the eye and said: 'So Year Seven was a really tough year for me. I didn't know anyone, and I spent a lot of the first term by myself. It sucked a lot.'

This wasn't the story I was expecting from Sophie. Miss Popular hadn't always been so popular. I looked at her with a sense of, *Okay, tell me more.*

She took a deep breath in between chews and continued.

'You'll meet lots of different people in this school. Some of them will be nice to you; some of them won't at first. But you're all stuck with each other for the next five years. Learn not to take everything personally . . .

'. . . and join an after-school club. I know it sounds

boring, but that's how you make friends and get to know people outside the classroom without annoying teachers breathing down your neck.

'Any questions for me?' she said, looking over my shoulder at the door. I could tell she had somewhere else to be.

'Nope, gotcha – thanks,' I said.

'Cool, here's my ChatBack username – follow me, and if you have any issues holla me whenever.'

And, just like that, she scribbled on a piece of paper, stood up and walked out. Everyone else's buddies were still answering all their questions. I guess Sophie had cracked the code at Archbishop Academy and felt she'd told me all I needed to know.

For sure, she doesn't spend lunchtimes all by herself any more. She has lots of friends – she's Sophie Walker after all. The most popular girl in Year 9, and she's my buddy.

After she had gone that day, I thought about what she'd said about us all being stuck with each other for the next five years. I looked round my new class and thought, *Yeah, she's right. Urgh.*

50

Anyway, that was last year, and this year feels much more bearable. I have Ade now, and gosh, she makes everything in this school okay.

CHAPTER 7
CHATBACK

@PrincessSuperAde: Omg, I left my English folder on the bus! Do you have today's notes?

> **@_Shannyxo:** Yeah, I'll bring them in for you tomorrow.

@PrincessSuperAde: Lifesaver! Thanks, Shanice xxx

> **@_Shannyxo:** Lol you're welcome, Princess Super Ade!

@PrincessSuperAde: Hahaha. Oh gosh. It's a nickname my dad gave me when I was little. I never could choose whether I wanted to be a princess or a superhero when it was World Book Day or Halloween or something fancy dress, so he bought me a cape and a tiara and made me his 'Princess Super Ade' :')

@PrincessSuperAde: It's kinda lame but I still like it. It reminds me of him. I don't see him as much these days.

                        @_Shannyxo: That's sad. Why not?

@PrincessSuperAde: I guess because he and my mum aren't together any more. He just stopped bothering as much. Once they broke up, it's like he broke up with all of us.

        @_Shannyxo: I'm sorry, Ade :(That is really rough.

@PrincessSuperAde: Made rougher by Mum trying to make her new boyfriend our new dad too. Sick of it.

                    @_Shannyxo: Oh no, is he that bad?

@PrincessSuperAde: The worst. He tries to be my mate all the time and won't leave me alone. It's bad enough Mum falls for the nice-guy act, but so do Bisi and Funmi. I don't even refer to him by his name. He's just *him* to me.

@_Shannyxo: My dad is an idiot half the time, tbh. Most are, at least sometimes. Even if your stepdad isn't your favourite person, I guess the fact he makes the effort counts for something?

@PrincessSuperAde: He tries too hard though.

@_Shannyxo: I hear you, but I guess that can be better than nothing? Like with your actual dad?

@PrincessSuperAde: Hmmm. Maybe. Maybe if it was anyone else but him :')

@_Shannyxo: Looool.

@PrincessSuperAde: I hate the way he tries to act like he's part of the family. Taking Mum away first and now my sisters.

@_Shannyxo: You still have your mum. She's not gone anywhere. She's still there for you.

@PrincessSuperAde: Omg I'm sorry, Shanice :(I can't even imagine how difficult that is, your mum being . . . I should have thought before I said that, sorry.

> **@_Shannyxo:** No, no! It's okay. I know you didn't mean anything by it. I just meant that it's not something to take for granted.

@PrincessSuperAde: I know. You're right. I hope you're okay?

> **@_Shannyxo:** I am, thanks. It can just be hard, you know? Some days more than others. Today is a hard day.

@PrincessSuperAde: Do you want to talk about it? I'm always here when you want to talk <3

> **@_Shannyxo:** Nah. Just happy I have someone to talk to about it if I need to :) Thanks for not making it awkward.

@PrincessSuperAde: :)

Chapter 8
Shanice

Hey,

I nearly missed the bus today because I couldn't find my new jumper so I almost had to take James's old school jumper again, which was not what I wanted to wear today of all days.

It's picture day, urgh. I always hate picture day. I really don't understand the fuss. Why do we have to take a photo at the beginning of every school year? It's one thing having to go to school every day, but it's quite another to have to smile and look happy about it.

Picture day is such a drag because everyone just does the most. The girls have fresh braids, cornrows or a blow-dry, and the guys have the trimmest cuts. I didn't even tell Dad about it because he would have made me take out my hair at the weekend and do a fresh set of braids. Hell no to that. If there's one thing I dread, it's sitting for ages, getting my hair done. There was one time I was there for hours – and I mean hours. It was so boring.

But today is different. Ade is going to be around. Normally, I really don't care what I wear, but I noticed she looks pretty cool at school. She was wearing some lip gloss the other day. I'm not a make-up girl at all. I see lots of the older girls at Archbishop Academy wearing it, and some of them just look ridiculous. I think they do it to impress boys. If there's one boy I do know well, it's James. Why you'd actually try and impress people like him puzzles me!

But today is picture day, and I might just make a little bit of effort. I still have a small stash of leftover make-up from a magazine Dad got for me a few months ago. Once in a while, he tries to bribe me into helping him out in the shop so he promises me this mag I quite like. It's called *Lauren's Secrets* and always has a few treats attached to it. Nail-art pens, roll-on body glitter, eyeshadows. Apart from the mag being full of glitter that gets everywhere and smelling like sugar, I do enjoy the trendy craft ideas. But some of the stuff is ridiculous: last week's issue had a quiz called: *How to know if a boy really likes you.* Not sure I'm gonna need that . . .

I still have a cherry lip gloss though from the last issue. It smells so, so, so good. I stood in front of the mirror in Mum and Dad's room and put some on, and my lips went from dry to luscious and dreamy. I moved on to my chunky braids. I tried to do something with them. When I say try . . . I really mean try because it did not go to plan. How do people manage this every day? No wonder my dad gets paid to do it for people.

I began by parting my braids in the way Mum showed me. After dividing my hair into four sections, I tied it up how Mum did, but I ended up looking like an overgrown pineapple. The hairband snapped, and I yelped in pain because it hurt really bad. Dad ran up the stairs and saw me sitting there, rubbing my hand.

He gave me a sympathetic smile. 'What's happened now?' he said.

I struggled to get my words out. 'I was trying to do my hair, but the hairband snapped and . . .'

Dad didn't even allow me to finish – he already had his hands on my hair. 'You were doing a good job – it's just that this hairband you're using is too thin.'

I closed my eyes while he did my hair, like when I was little. A few minutes later, he tapped me on the shoulder, and I looked in the mirror. He'd transformed my disaster into something I loved. I tried not to smile too much.

I stared at myself for a few seconds, 'Thanks, Dad. It's picture day today.' I felt the need to explain.

'Ah, I see. That comes round sooner than I remember these days,' he said.

'Yeah, usually I don't care, as you know, but I wanted to impress Ade. You see, she . . .'

Dad stopped me before I could finish.

'Shanice, you don't have to impress anyone. People will be drawn to you for who you are, and you don't have

to change into anything you're not comfortable with.'

'I guess. It's just so hard sometimes because, deep down, I'm happy not to fit in, and I can just do my own thing, but I also want to be liked sometimes . . . you know?'

'I know. Trust me, I know. However, never lose sight of what makes you special by morphing into someone you're not. It's no fun. That's why I loved your mother so much. She was a real individual – you take after her.'

Before I could say anything, James barged in and started to have a go at me for making him late.

'If you're not ready on time, I'm going without you – it really isn't my responsibility.'

'Oh yes, it is,' Dad said.

Dad always insists James walks me to the stop, and we get the bus together. He grumpily agrees, but complains that I'm old enough to walk on my own. He's right. I am old enough. I know he can't wait till he goes to sixth form next year and is off the hook.

'Okay, but can we go now? The boys are waiting for me . . .' he mumbled. The boys. James's best friends – I call them the clones. It's like one of him isn't enough!

I caught a glimpse of myself in the mirror as I rushed

out of the front door. Dad did well.

As we walked to the bus stop, I noticed James had made an effort today too. The stylish gene may have skipped me, but James was super cool. Today he was wearing some new trainers. His jumper was tucked in, and a little bit of his shirt was showing. Not too much, just enough for teachers not to care and enough for him to be seen as a rebel among his friends.

He always insists I walk three steps in front of him so that he can see I'm okay, but far enough away not to cramp his style. I'm not allowed to acknowledge him once we leave the house 'unless there's an emergency', he says. Typical pain of a big brother.

We got to school just before the second bell went. As I scanned the hall for Ade, Mr Oppong appeared, looking cross. 'Shanice, as you know, today is picture day, and we're running a tight ship.'

'I know, sir. I was just looking . . .'

'You're already late so you don't have the liberty to be *just looking* for anyone . . .'

He really does annoy me. 'Yes, sir,' I whispered.

I dash into class before he gives me a detention. Ade comes in just after me – I'm relieved to see her.

'Your hair looks so nice. It really suits you like that,' she says.

'Thanks!' I can't stop grinning.

My finger almost snapping off painfully was worth it, then!

'So today is picture day, eh? In my old school, nobody made much of an effort.'

'Yeah, Archbishop Academy is trying to build up its reputation so picture day has become a big thing around here.'

'I can see that.' She gestures to one of the girls opposite us.

She's sitting there, looking very uncomfortable, her hair pulled back into an incredibly tight, sleek ponytail, her baby hair

gelled to perfection

and every button on her shirt done up, making her look like a robot with no personality. I try not to giggle. She's a nice girl, but I do wonder what her parents were thinking.

'Yeah, not sure what's going on there,' I whisper to Ade.

Ade looks great too, but then she always does, so that's nothing new. She's wearing a new pair of earrings I haven't seen before. I wonder if they are Bisi's. Unlike Mrs P, Mr Oppong is less fussed about things like that.

After Mr Oppong takes the register, we chat while we wait for the morning announcements. By the time we get up to go to the main hall for the photo, the whole class is buzzing with excitement. I'm small for my age, so I'm always put at the front for school pictures. I lose Ade to another row when Mr Oppong asks her to stand next to the Double-A girls. Another reason to be annoyed at him – why would he go out of his way to move her next to them?

Then I see Double A talking to Ade. My stomach starts to feel a little pang. I know I'm not hungry – I ate all of my porridge this morning. I'm not worried she's going to prefer them. How could she? Ade is my friend.

I just don't want them corrupting her. They're not nice girls like her. Now I see Aaliyah whispering into Ade's ear, and Ade starts laughing really hard. I wonder what can be so funny.

Chapter 9

Ade

Dear Diary,

WHY IS MY LIFE SO UNFAIR? Things were actually going great, but today was such a drag. We're decorating the house, and I was supposed to go shopping with Mum and Funmi to pick the paint colours for our bedroom. But then Mum insisted I go with *him*, even though I said that I'd rather eat broccoli (my least favourite food) and wash it down with prune juice (my least favourite drink).

'Why can't I just go with you?' I wailed.

'Ade, I thought Funmi was the baby of the house,' Mum teased. 'Don't throw a tantrum!'

'I'm not. I just thought today was going to be you

and me,' I said, sticking out my bottom lip in a strop.

'There's plenty of time for that, but I've got to take Funmi to her karate class and then go to the shops to get something for supper. Now stop being silly, and go and give your stepdad a hand.' I could hear the annoyance creeping into her voice, but still I pushed.

'I don't see why I should have to go and not Bisi,' I grumbled, crossing my arms. 'Why am I being picked on?'

'I know you think the world revolves round you, my dear, but you are not being picked on,' Mum said sarcastically. 'Bisi helped me with the shopping last week, as well as being kind enough to help Emmanuel fix the Wi-Fi. So I'll ask you one more time: help your stepdad with choosing the paint or no pocket money this week.'

'But that's so unfair!'

'Tough. Ade, I'm asking you to do this not because I'm picking on you, but because it's an important job, and it's supposed to be fun! I thought you might enjoy it.'

'Well, you thought wrong,' I muttered under my breath.

'What did you say?' Mum's neck snapped round like a hawk.

'I said you're never wrong! Gosh, Mum.'

'That's what I thought.' Mum smiled. 'Now get going, or you'll be late back!'

The ride in the car was torture. We're miles away from the local shopping centre, so it took us nearly an hour to get there. An hour of *him* making small talk, and me doing everything I could to send the clearest possible message that he was my least favourite person on the planet. But the guy is stupid; he can't take a hint.

I'd give *him* **one-word answers**, sometimes **no answer at all**, but he'd still keep yammering on.

Even worse, my headphones are broken so my plan to drown *him* out with my favourite music didn't exactly work. I tried putting them on just to pretend, so he'd leave me alone, but, like the socially awkward weirdo that he is, he pointed out the fact that they weren't working!

'Your mum says you're in the market for new ones,' he said, smiling. 'I have a pretty good pair that I bought last year. I don't get much use out of them any more. They're yours if you want.'

Offering me his second-hand leftovers that have been all over his big hairy ears? No thanks!

'I don't want,' I replied, looking out of the window. 'I don't do sloppy seconds.'

He laughed. He actually laughed, although I was being dead serious. You see why I can't stand him?

'Well, we could pick some up today if you like?' he said.

'Whatever.' I shrugged.

'Just don't tell your mum. I'm sure she'd kill me if she knew I was getting you a brand-new pair before you've tried mine.'

'Why do you want me to keep secrets from Mum?' I snapped back. 'You can keep your dodgy headphones.'

'It was a joke, Ade,' he said weakly. 'Come on, lighten up a little bit!'

'Don't tell me what to do,' I said. I was properly angry now. 'You're not my dad, and you never will be.'

It just came flying out, the words ringing out in the silent car before I realised I'd said them. He took a deep breath and sighed, before pulling over to the side of the road. What had I done? Now he wanted to have

a 'talk'.

'Ade, I know I'm not your dad,' he said. I could see his eyes in the rear-view mirror and he looked like he might cry — how sad is that? 'I'm not trying to be your dad. I never would. But your mum and I have been together three years now. And I do love her and you girls, whether you like it or not. And I hope we can have a friendship when you're ready.'

'A friendship? Why would I want a friendship with you?' I shouldn't have bothered replying, but I couldn't stop myself. 'It's all your fault we had to leave. My school, my mates, my aunty, my dad. All of it. We're stuck in this boring old town where we don't know anyone, just because you wanted to come here.'

'I didn't want to, Ade — I had to. We had to. If the

same job had come up in our old area, I would have taken it, but unfortunately that's not how things worked out. You'll understand better when you're older.'

I hate it when adults say that. I'll get it when I'm older. Because I know I won't; what's right is right, and what's wrong is wrong, and *him* taking me away from the things I care about won't suddenly make sense when I hit his age.

It sucks, however you slice it.

'I am sorry that it worked out this way, but I'm glad you appear to be making lots of new friends at school. Hopefully, that makes up for things a bit.'

'*No. It doesn't,*' I said, looking out of the window, thinking of my dad.

He started the car up again, and we drove the rest of the way in complete silence. When we got to the shopping centre, I spoke up again.

'I don't want to get out of the car,' I said, crossing my arms.

He smiled a sad smile. 'I understand. You can text me any colour ideas you have if you like.' I nodded, still looking away.

'And I know you don't like to even joke about not telling your mum things,' he said, 'but I won't tell her about this if you won't.'

I said nothing. And, when he left to buy the paint, I didn't text him a thing, of course.

A little while later, he got back in the car, looking miserable, so I finally had some peace — pure, blissful silence on the drive back home. Why he's so desperate to pretend we're mates, I'll never know. Just because Mum likes *him* doesn't mean I have to. That's one thing they can't make me do.

Chapter 10
Shanice

Hey,

I still don't know what to call you. Because you're not exactly a diary, are you? Ade says I should give you a name – I don't know though. Seems a bit odd calling you something you haven't agreed to. It's like when people call me Shan for short. I'm like, urgh, go away. I'm not your Shan. My name is Shanice, thanks! I'm very picky when it comes to names.

There was a friend of Mum's who kept calling me Shar. 'Darling Shar . . .' 'My baby Shar . . .' 'Shar the princess . . .' It made me cringe so bad. She was one of those really loud aunties too – you'd hear her before you saw her – and I made every effort to avoid seeing her.

When I say 'aunty', she's not like my mum's sister or Dad's sister or anything like that. It's what we have to call Mum's and Dad's friends when they're around, because it's rude to use their first name. I really don't understand why. These rules and regulations just never make sense. Dad says it's to show you respect them. Well, maybe if she respected me and called me by my actual name, then I'd have no problem 'respecting' her.

But come on: who gave you permission to shorten my name? This 'aunty' got me a present one day with Shar written on the wrapping paper and gave it to me with a big smile on her face. I tried to show her how unimpressed I felt, but Mum gave me a look, and I had to fake a smile and say how grateful I was.

Luckily for this aunty, her gift was pretty sick, so I didn't have to fake a smile for long. She'd got me these headphones I'd wanted for ages, but Mum had said were too pricey. They were, of course, pink (*yaass*), but a real nice metallic pink (I'm starting to think this is my fave

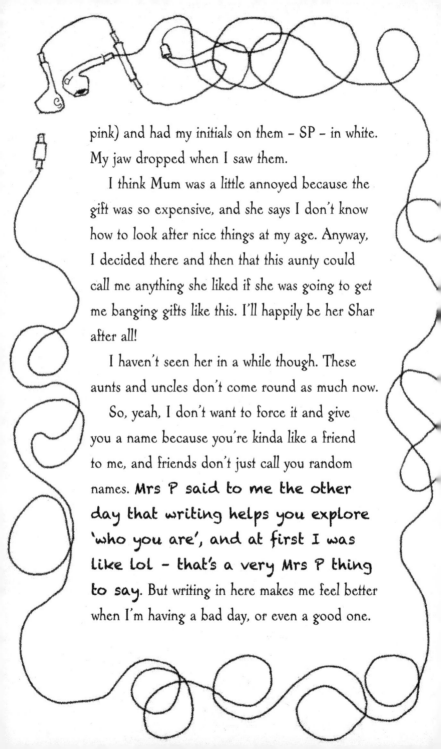

pink) and had my initials on them – SP – in white.
My jaw dropped when I saw them.

I think Mum was a little annoyed because the
gift was so expensive, and she says I don't know
how to look after nice things at my age. Anyway,
I decided there and then that this aunty could
call me anything she liked if she was going to get
me banging gifts like this. I'll happily be her Shar
after all!

I haven't seen her in a while though. These
aunts and uncles don't come round as much now.

So, yeah, I don't want to force it and give
you a name because you're kinda like a friend
to me, and friends don't just call you random
names. **Mrs P said to me the other
day that writing helps you explore
'who you are', and at first I was
like lol – that's a very Mrs P thing
to say.** But writing in here makes me feel better
when I'm having a bad day, or even a good one.

I love sharing those moments with you – it's like talking to a friend every single day, and I can say whatever I want with no guilt or repercussions.

Anyway, time for bed! I like waking up really early these days, so I don't miss Ade at the school gates. It's been really cool walking into class with someone. It's like we have our own lil double act going on.

Chapter 11

Ade

OMG, OMG, OMGGGG! Today was so, so cool!

THIS MORNING, *HE* WENT TO WORK SUPER EARLY, SO IT WAS JUST ME, MUM, FUNMI AND BISI, EXACTLY LIKE OLD TIMES. Mum made us huge plates of yam and egg for breakfast (my favourite), and Bisi wasn't even in a mood or anything today so things must be going well with her latest boyfriend (for now). We spent all morning in our pj's, watching cartoons — Mum wasn't even on at us about homework or anything. It was the first time this house had really felt like *home*.

The best bit didn't come till the afternoon.

:::
And that was . . . wait for it . . . a surprise visit from my favourite person in the world, my **Aunty Kim!**
:::

She came at around twelve, disrupting our lunchtime and bringing all the colours of the rainbow with her as always — a blue baseball cap over her short auburn pixie cut, a yellow scarf, a red jacket and orange leggings paired with bright green trainers. She came with treats as usual — carrier bags that I knew would be heaving with chocolates, sweets and fizzy drinks. I was in the toilet, where I'd been scrolling ChatBack, when I heard her chattering away with Mum and making Funmi even more hyper than usual.

'WHERE'S MY ADE?' she boomed from the kitchen.

That's one of the best things about Aunty Kim — she doesn't even bother to pretend I'm not her favourite. I ran down the stairs and jumped on her, hugging her as tight as I could. I'd missed her so much, and hugging her felt like embracing everything we'd left behind.

'You're messing up my hair, girl!' she said, her voice muffled by my arms. 'And my make-up!'

I clambered off her and peered at her face. Sure enough, her bright pink lippy and blusher were slightly smudged, but her lilac eyeshadow was intact. I looked down at the bags.

'Yes, yes, I come bearing gifts,' she said with a smirk. 'Plenty of time for that later, but first you need to tell me all about school and your writing!'

'Not much to report,' I said, taking the bags from her and putting them on the kitchen table. 'Nothing like my old school, nowhere near as good.'

'Oh, come on, Ade, you're not still sulking about the move, are you?' she said, nudging my arm. 'I'm sure a chatterbox like you has made loads of new friends by now.'

Mum butted in. 'She has. Go on, Ade, tell her about the new friend you made before you'd even started school!'

'I guess I did make a mate,' I said with a shrug.

'I knew it!' Aunty Kim smiled. 'Tell me all about it!'

So I told her about Shanice, how we'd met when Mum was getting her hair done at Powers, how she'd been writing in the same big pink diary as me and put up with Funmi's bogey flicking and everything.

'I like the sound of this Shanice,' Aunty Kim said after a while. 'She seems smart. Like you!'

'She'll be round this afternoon, so you can see for yourself if you want.'

'Well, that's lucky for her,' she said with a grin. 'Since I'm taking you and your sister on a shopping spree!'

'SHOPPPPINGGGG!'

Funmi came in from nowhere, bundling into Aunty Kim's lap. I swear she has selective hearing — she can't hear when she's being told to do something, but is all ears when it comes to food or fun.

'Yes, shopping.' Aunty Kim laughed. 'Your aunty got lucky on the lotto this week, and she's feeling generous . . . that is, if it's okay with Mum?'

We all looked at Mum with our biggest, most innocent eyes. 'Hmm. I thought Shanice was coming over to help with homework . . .' Mum began, hand on hip.

'I promise we'll finish it as soon as we get back.' I gave her a pleading look. 'Aunty Kim can drop me at hers afterwards, and we'll work extra hard. Come on, Mum. We haven't seen Aunty Kim in ages!'

'Yes, come on, Mum — we'll be back by three at the very latest!' Aunty Kim said.

We all pouted at Mum. She sighed and reached for her handbag. Pulling out her car keys, she handed them to her sister. 'Fine, fine. But you girls better be back by three, you hear? Can't have you hogging Aunty Kim all to yourselves — she and I have stuff to catch up on too!'

'Yes, Mum!' Funmi and I said, already at the door, grabbing our coats.

'And no sweets for Funmi before dinner!' she called after us.

'Of course not!' Aunty Kim said with a wink,

popping a purple Skittle in Funmi's hand and holding her finger to her lips.

I messaged Shanice that we were on our way to pick her up.

Who's we?

Me, Funmi and my fave person ever.

Your Aunty Kim is visiting?

She already knows me so well!

Shanice lives above the hairdresser's, so we had to go round to the back entrance to reach her flat. We pressed the bell and, when her dad answered the door, Aunty Kim's eyes lit up like a Christmas tree. 'Well, hello . . . Mr Powers, is it?'

'Yeah, but you can call me Matthew,' he said with a smile. 'You must be Ade's Aunty Kim. Shanice told me you'd be picking her up.'

'Oh, please,' she said, holding out her hand for him to shake, speaking in a weird posh voice I only heard her use when people called from the bank. 'Kim is just fine.'

At that moment, Shanice came out from under her dad's arm, dressed in a dark blue T-shirt and jeans.

'And this must be Shanice! Lovely to meet you!' said Aunty Kim. 'I've heard lots about you!'

'I've heard loads about you too from Ade,' Shanice replied.

'All good, I hope?' Aunty Kim asked. 'In fact, don't answer that till your dad's gone.'

Matthew laughed and turned to Shanice. 'Now I don't want you causing any trouble for Aunty Kim, you hear?'

'Yes, Dad,' Shanice said, making her way to the car.

'Don't worry, Matthew – you go and relax. See you soon!' Aunty Kim said in her weird posh voice.

When we were in the car, she was smiling to herself. She turned round in her seat to face us. 'Tell me, Shanice, is your dad single?'

Shanice and I tried not to laugh. 'I think so . . . why?' she replied.

'Don't worry about it,' said Aunty Kim, still smiling as we bit the insides of our cheeks. 'Just good to know.'

We got to the shopping centre a while later and honestly? It was probably the most fun I've had in ages. Even though there aren't as many shops here as in our old town, everything's fun with Aunty Kim.

While Funmi ran around like a lunatic, Aunty Kim and I started styling Shanice. She loves the colour pink, but that's where her relationship with anything girly begins and ends — we had to convince her to try on anything sparkly. We tried on so many different outfits and shoes, and, when we made it to the accessories, a pair of blue hoops were glittering in my eyeline.

'These are Bisi's earrings!' I said, running over to them. 'The ones Mrs P confiscated from me in English!'

'The ones that Aaliyah said were "unreal", Shanice said, pulling a face.

'I know. How weird was that? She barely even acknowledged my existence when she said it!'

'Typical Double-A behaviour,' Shanice said, crossing her arms. 'Even when they give a compliment, it's somehow still rude.'

'What's a Double A?' Aunty Kim said, getting in between us. 'Your nosy Aunty Kim wants to hear all the goss!'

'Just these girls at our school. Well, these mean,

popular girls at school,' Shanice said.

Kim nodded. 'There's a group like that at every school. They're not trying anything with my baby Ade, are they?'

'No,' I said. 'Well, not yet anyway. But Shanice has had trouble with them before, haven't you?'

'Yeah, well, most kids at Archbishop Academy have if they're not considered "cool" enough by them.

Amy made Ellie Wright cry on her birthday, and Aaliyah put a stink bomb in Jacob Owens's locker.

'But, because I never had any interest in being their mate, they've always had it in for me in particular. They hide my PE kit, whisper and snigger whenever I answer questions in class. They called me "Shanice Never Showers" for the first few months of Year Seven because I wore the same top twice on ChatBack.'

'Gosh,' Aunty Kim said, looking worried. 'They sound terrible!'

'They are.'

'Well, I'm glad you got to Ade before they did,' Aunty Kim said. 'Because girls like that tend to draw you into their gang and try to make you just like them.'

Aunty Kim bought me the earrings so I could replace them before Bisi noticed. ('And then you can keep the original pair once Mrs P returns them at the end of term!' she said.)

For Funmi, she picked up a cuddly toy frog (Funmi specifically wanted a frog, over every other animal — she is the WEIRDEST) and even bought Shanice a cute pink top she'd been looking at. Then she got us all soft cinnamon pretzels and bottles of Coke. She didn't make me or Funmi split a large or anything!

By the time she drove us back to Shanice's to do our homework, Funmi had already fallen asleep.

'Thanks for the T-shirt, Aunty Kim!' Shanice said, hopping out of the car.

'You're welcome. And tell your dad I send my best, yeah?'

Before I got out, we had a cuddle, and Aunty Kim held on to me. 'Shanice is a lovely girl,' she whispered. 'A good friend for sure. I'm happy you've got each other.'

'Yeah,' I agreed. 'She's the best.'

'Those other girls don't seem to be very nice to her, do they?'

'Double A? They don't get along,' I said sadly.

'Well, that's a shame. It sounds like they can be quite mean. Whatever you do, make sure you don't leave her out, even if you do become mates with them, yeah? Seems like they may have taken a shine to you.'

'Oh, come on, Aunty,' I scoffed. 'One of them only said she liked my earrings.'

'Well, from girls that are best known for being mean, I wouldn't take it for granted. Be careful, yeah? And always have Shanice's back. She's a good kid.'

'Obviously!' I said, before running to join my friend. 'See you when I get home!'

Aunty Kim can be a bit patronising at times. As if Double A would want anything to do with me, or me with them. And obviously I'd never leave Shanice out. **She's my best mate!**

CHAPTER 12

CHATBACK

@PrincessSuperAde: Heyyyyy, girl, how's it going? x

@_Shannyxo: I've been waiting for you to come online all day!!

@PrincessSuperAde: Loool, really why?

@_Shannyxo: Because I think I'm getting a bearded dragon after all this time!

@PrincessSuperAde: Omg omg, the one you wanted from Petsland??!

@_Shannyxo: Yes, that exact one!

@PrincessSuperAde: I'd love to see it!! When you say think, you mean your dad finally came round?

> **@_Shannyxo:** Oh, so here's the thing. I overheard him on the phone and I think he was talking to Ms Davies, the owner, and something about making it a surprise and how I deserve it!

@PrincessSuperAde: Awww that's so cute!

> **@_Shannyxo:** Yeaaaah, I really deserve it. I've been so good recently – I've been washing up when it wasn't my day and even helping out sorting the laundry.

@PrincessSuperAde: Wowza, you've really been putting the work in, haven't you? Haha!

> **@_Shannyxo:** Loool, yesss, and it all paid off – but once I get her I'm totally gonna stop tehehehe, back to my old ways! Your Aunty Kim was so much fun yesterday.

@PrincessSuperAde: Yeah, she's really the best, sorry about her being weird about your dad lol.

@_Shannyxo: Loooool, that's all right. I've noticed these women get like that in the shop. It's as if they're all trying to audition to be my new mum or something.

@PrincessSuperAde: That must be super weird.

@_Shannyxo: Yeah, it is because no one can be my new mum. That's not how things work!

@PrincessSuperAde: Yeah, soz. Aunty Kim can be very full on at times. Mum says she's a free spirit, speaks first and thinks later and all that.

@_Shannyxo: Looool, she's fun, I like her a lot. If there's anybody that I wouldn't mind having around it would be her.

@PrincessSuperAde: Omg that would make us like family if that happened. Could you imagine – we would be like what? Cousins or something?

> @_Shannyxo: Yesss, I think so – that would be so
> much fun. We'd be friends AND family :)

@PrincessSuperAde: We're kinda like sisters already.
You're like my non-identical twin loool. We're same
same but different, you know?

> @_Shannyxo: Loool, that's so true. I've always
> wanted a sister.

@PrincessSuperAde: :) <3

> @_Shannyxo: Omg a sibling I do not want . . . James
> is calling me for dinner. G2G. See ya later, girl xx

@PrincessSuperAde: Same with me. Bisi says it's time
for dinner too, bye, girl xx

Ade

Dear Diary,
YOU COULDN'T GUESS WHAT HAPPENED TO ME TODAY
IF I PAID YOU.

So, obviously, me and Shanice are like best friends already, right? Well, I think I'm going to have two other joint best friends too (which would mean I have three best friends at once — a personal record!). And you will NOT believe who they are.

Shanice was off sick today (though I'm going to have to ask her about the fact that her symptoms coincidentally started around the time the history quiz was announced lol . . .), so I'm sitting alone during registration, wondering how I'm going to survive the rest of the day. Mr Oppong does the register and, when we get to the end, our tutor group starts getting ready for lessons.

My first class is physics with Mrs Buchanan — and you know how bad I am at physics — so I'm scribbling down some last-minute answers to the homework I might have forgotten to finish last night. So far so normal. That is until Amy Parker and Aaliyah Saleem start walking in my direction and pull up a chair at my table. I was so confused — I nearly moved out of their way because I was sure they'd made some sort of mistake.

They were rocking matching high ponytails, Amy's haystack blonde locks and Aaliyah's thick, black, back-length hair scraped up with bright red scrunchies that matched our bright red jumpers and ties. They always manage to make our dusty old boring uniform look cool — I heard Amy gets her trousers from that trendy new shop that's opened on the high street instead of the 'Archbishop Academy approved outlets'. Aaliyah apparently borrows her sister's pricey trainers — she's on her fourth and final warning from Mr Oppong about it, but she doesn't care. (Bisi would never lend me her trainers. Or anything. So unfair!)

'Hey, new girl,' Amy said, flicking her blonde ponytail over her shoulder. 'You want to walk with us to physics?'

I looked around to make sure she was talking to me.

'Yes, you,' Aaliyah laughed. 'You're the only new girl here, right?'

I nodded.

'Right! So do you want to or what?'

I nodded again.

'Does she actually speak?' Aaliyah said, rolling her eyes. 'I knew this was a bad idea.'

'I do speak!' I squeaked more than said.

'See?' Amy smiled smugly at Aaliyah. 'I know what I'm doing. She has potential!'

The walk to physics was like the longest minute of my life. It felt as if I was being interviewed for something. They kept asking me questions: what my favourite colour was; who was my favourite singer; who was the best-looking boy in the school (easy — I've only been here two weeks and even I know it's Kyle Teixeira in Year 9).

Well, I'm not sure how, but I seemed to pass their weird test because, ever since, they've been treating me like I'm the third member of their gang. When we got to physics, we all went our separate ways and sat in our allocated seats, and I thought that was it; I was pretty sure they were going to act like no one existed outside of their duo. And I was fine with that — me and Shanice are our own double act. But, halfway through the lesson, Jacob Owens passed a note to Gemma Osborne who passed it on to Katie Oliver who passed it to me. I opened it: it was from Aaliyah.

Sit with us this lunchtime!! xox

I thought about what Shanice had said about them. How they'd been so mean to her. Then I thought about eating lunch alone like the new-girl loser loner at Archbishop Academy. How rude it would be to say no to what was just a friendly gesture. I wrote back.

Okay. See you at ten past twelve!

When I got to the lunch hall, sure enough, there they were, each with an identical plate of vegetable goujons and chips. I had got myself a huge uncool helping of sausage and mash, and sat down with them.

'Hey,' I said nervously.

'Oh, hey,' said Aaliyah. They were huddling over something under the table. 'You all right?'

'I'm good,' I smiled. 'What are you guys looking at?'

Amy glanced at me and then back down to her lap as a signal. I peered closer. It was a mobile phone — a really expensive one too! How she managed to sneak it in I have no idea, as there's a very strict no-phones policy at Archbishop. A video was playing, showing Amy and Aaliyah doing a dance routine. They were good. *Really* good.

'I got seven hundred and eighty-six likes on our last post of us dancing on ChatBack!' Amy said after a while.

I think she saw how my jaw dropped and smiled smugly. 'Isn't that unreal?'

'Not bad,' Aaliyah said, inspecting her nails. 'But on my page it was up to eight hundred and six last time I checked. May even have gone up more by now.'

Amy mock-yawned at her, and they started to laugh.

'I'm lucky if I even hit double figures on mine!' I said.

'Keep hanging out with us and that will soon change,' said Amy with a wink. 'Can you dance?'

'I love dancing!' I said. I'm pretty good at it too, though definitely not in their league.

'Great! You should definitely record some videos with me and Aaliyah some time after school. That would be unreal!' Amy said.

I smiled widely, unable to hide my excitement.

'So how are you finding it at Archbishop?' asked

Aaliyah, batting a goujon around her plate with her fork. 'You like it?'

'It's okay,' I said. 'Still trying to find my feet.'

'You'll get there soon enough. Isn't Mrs P, the English teaching assistant, the absolute *worst*?' Amy said, sticking her tongue out. 'Never met a woman so nosy!'

I laughed. 'Yeah, I'm definitely not a fan. My friend Shanice really gets on with her though. I guess I might see why at some point.'

They looked at each other. 'Shanice Powers?' said Aaliyah, scrunching up her face. 'The one who always sits alone and scribbles in that big pink book of hers?'

'Yeah!' I smiled. 'I met her before I came here, at her dad's hairdresser's. She's great!'

'Yeah ... she's not really our cup of tea,' Amy said, pulling a face. 'I'm not sure if you've noticed, but we're a pretty big deal around here? And we're super selective about who we hang out with.'

At this, Aaliyah stretched her arm out in front of my nose as she held up Amy's wrist. On both were braided friendship bracelets, Amy's turquoise,

Aaliyah's purple, with a gold A pendant hanging from each one. 'We have loads of mates, but the Double As are exclusive. Shanice is a bit . . .' Her voice trailed off.

'Anyway, we should definitely hang out together,' Amy interjected. 'You're definitely more up our street.'

My last three periods were geography, history and Spanish, which were all okay (I tell a lie — history was *boringggg*) and then it was back to tutor group. As I approached my locker to get my bag, Amy and Aaliyah were there waiting for me.

'Walk with us to the bus stop?' Amy said.

'Sure!' I replied.

They linked arms with me as we made our way there.

'See you tomorrow, Ade!' they said together when we reached the bus stop. I made sure not to tell them my mum was picking me up. When I got round the corner, I nearly didn't get in the car because *he* was sitting in the driver's seat.

'Sorry, Ade — your mum had to run some errands,

so it's me today,' he said apologetically.

'I don't see why I can't just get the bus like everyone else,' I said under my breath.

'I can have a chat with your mum about it if you like? You've been at Archbishop a while now, and I'm sure she'd be fine with it, especially if you're going to school with Shanice.'

'Whatever.' I sighed.

Gosh, he was always sucking up. Still, at least he didn't say much during the car ride.

Silver
linings.

That evening, I got friend requests from both Amy and Aaliyah on ChatBack. Their screen names were @DoubleAmy and @DoubleAaliyah, and they had *tons* of followers. Their pages were so grown-up and fashionable — plus, they're such sick dancers. My profile seemed pretty embarrassing by comparison —

I had to delete a couple of cringe pictures before I accepted their requests. I know Shanice isn't a huge fan of theirs, but they were really nice to me! I hope we can all hang out together as a group — we'd rule the school!

I did see something that gave me pause. I scrolled all the way back on Amy's page, past all the flawless selfies and dance routines, and saw a picture of someone who wasn't her or Aaliyah or any of the handful of girls in our year they seemed to be 'friends' with. It was a picture of Shanice, taken from her profile. She was dressed in a cute T-shirt and jeans, smiling more broadly than usual. They'd drawn flies and stink lines coming off her and captioned it #NeverShowersPowers. Aaliyah was at the top of the comments, crying with laughter at it too!

I was a bit taken aback — no surprise that Shanice had been right about Double A. They really could be mean. I can't lie — it did make me a little bit wary. But this was a while ago — you can't hold people's past mistakes against them forever, right? So I'm hoping things have changed, and that they've grown up since then. We're in Year 8 now. Besides, I haven't seen any more mean posts, not about Shanice anyway.

Now I have to finish my history homework (yuck) so got to go — will update you soon.

Chapter 14
Shanice

Hey,

You're probably wondering why I'm writing to you so early! It's because I've got a bit of a cold today. Yeah, I'm sick - sickly sick. Poor me, right? I was up all through the night and couldn't sleep and, when I went into Dad's room in the morning, he took my temperature, which confirmed I was indeed sick and not faking it this time.

'My head hurts, Dad,' I said, feeling very sorry for myself.

'Oh boy, you're burning up,' he said worriedly. I suddenly did feel ill, but it wasn't the kind of ill that you need to go to hospital for, just the sort that you need to get back into bed for.

He got me all sorts of things to make me feel better: butter-and-jam toast, my big blanket, special medicine from the cupboard and my fluffy pillow I've had since I was, like, three years old. I had a very cosy and peaceful morning, and soon I was feeling a bit better. I watched all my favourite TV shows without interruption, but then I got bored, like really bored. So I checked ChatBack, and of course no one was online because they were all at school.

I really don't like that app: it's basically a popularity contest, and everyone knows how that goes. I only got it because I was curious, as it seemed to be the talk of the school when I first started there. The Double-A girls apparently get the most likes, and everyone is just in awe of their silly dance routines. I refuse to go on their page, urgh. I don't get the hype with those girls, never have and never will. But I did finally add Sophie. Her page is everything you'd expect. She's posted so many selfies. Have I mentioned how pretty she is? I don't expect a follow-back from her though. She hardly follows anyone back. That's fine with me. She's my school buddy, but she's also the most popular girl in Year 9.

Anyway, I'm writing now because I've run out of things to watch, and I'm also feeling much better. But I won't be telling Dad that. He's the type to drive me to school if he suspects I'm playing it up.

There was a history quiz today – glad I'm missing out on that. I like history, but hate the quizzes. And yes, you guessed: history is boring at school. The teacher teaches it in such a way that I soon zone out and borderline fall asleep. I mean the whole class does. His voice is so dry, and he just seems to find it impossible to make the subject interesting, however hard he tries. So it wasn't until there was a supply teacher last year that I realised history could be quite fun. See, I hate group work where you're forced to team up with people: there's always that awkward scramble of who gets paired with who.

But, when this supply teacher split us up, he made us do some interactive role plays of the event he'd been teaching us about in history. It was hilarious watching everyone act out the characters, and at first I was reluctant to take part – I usually hate any form of performance, but once everyone had got into character I felt much more comfortable. My role was very minor anyway. I didn't have to say much – the other people in my group were happy to hog the limelight.

But then my teacher came back, and history got boring again. I complained to Mrs P one day after English, and, even though she isn't a history teacher, we often end up talking about the world and things that happened in the past.

'History isn't just the memorisation of people, places and dates, Shanice.'

'But then why do we have to get tested on it?' I said, confused.

'Because learning to think historically allows us to help people understand the events that happen today, and that may hopefully avoid bad things happening in the future.'

Hmm, okay. I just prefer to do my own reading for history now. Mrs P got me a book called *The Life and Reign of Queen Elizabeth I*. She was basically one of the most powerful women in British history. We'd started learning about her in class, and as predicted it had been a snoozefest. But, when I spent this afternoon reading Mrs P's book, I discovered that Elizabeth I was anything but boring. The portrait of her on the front cover made her look so powerful; her clothes and sparkling jewellery were so blingy – OMG. Her dad was Henry VIII, but she was only the second queen in English history to rule in her own right because in those days most people didn't believe a woman was fit to do so. But Elizabeth was quick to prove them

wrong! She's remembered for being a different kind of queen.

And that was the book I'd been reading when Dad came in and found me asleep on the sofa. A perfect sick day if you ask me.

CHAPTER 15
■
CHATBACK

@PrincessSuperAde: Hey! How are you doing? Hope you're feeling better :)

@_Shannyxo: Yeah, I am. Thanks :) Can I be honest? I played up my cold a bit so I could skip the history quiz, stay in and watch Netflix :'D

@PrincessSuperAde: Lol I KNEW IT! Anyway, you'll never guess who I made friends with today.

@_Shannyxo: Hmmm . . . Ellie Wright?

@PrincessSuperAde: Nope.

@_Shannyxo: Lakshmi Murthy?

@PrincessSuperAde: Cold.

@_Shannyxo: Jacob Owens?

@PrincessSuperAde: Getting colder!

@_Shannyxo: Paige Davies?

@PrincessSuperAde: FREEZING!

@_Shannyxo: I literally have no idea lol. Just tell me who.

@PrincessSuperAde: Okay, I will. But promise not to make a big deal out of it.

@_Shannyxo: Why would I? It's not like it's gonna be the Double As or anything.

@PrincessSuperAde: . . . It IS the Double As loool :D

@_Shannyxo: . . . Are you serious?

@PrincessSuperAde: I'm completely serious! Isn't that crazy?

@_Shannyxo: It's . . . definitely something!

@PrincessSuperAde: What do you mean? Are you annoyed at me :(?

@_Shannyxo: No lol. I'm a bit annoyed at them though, because why are they coming up to you and trying to be your friend? Weird, since they hate most people. But I'm not annoyed at you. Just at the situation. I hope you'll be careful around them.

@PrincessSuperAde: Of course I will!

@_Shannyxo: Because they'll probably try and make sure you're not friends with me any more, you know.

@PrincessSuperAde: As if. That would never work anyway!

@_Shannyxo: Hmm . . . whatever you say lol.

@PrincessSuperAde: You know you're always going to be my closest friend, right? Like I met you first, not them. We hung out and stuff today at lunch and it was fun, but you're my actual proper best friend.

@_Shannyxo: I mean, I hope so lol.

@PrincessSuperAde: Come on! You should know so!

@_Shannyxo: Lol yeah, yeah, I know so. It's not about you though. I trust you, I just don't trust them!

@PrincessSuperAde: Well, I'm glad you trust me at least :) I'm not going anywhere.

@_Shannyxo: Promise?

@PrincessSuperAde: Promise!

@_Shannyxo: Pinky swear?

@PrincessSuperAde: Pinky swear on the colour pink! <3

                              @_Shannyxo: Okay. Good :)

@PrincessSuperAde: Great :)

Chapter 16

Shanice

HEY!

Guess what?!

I had Ade round mine for a sleepover. I know, right? Okay, so let me tell you what went down and how I managed to convince my dad. He did take some convincing. Like a lot.

Dad was very reluctant because he kept on saying he had so much to do with the shop these days. He was short-staffed. He had to be around for deliveries. Blah-blah-blah. He's always so preoccupied these days. I hate it when he acts like he's so busy he can't do anything. It's not my fault.

He never seems to have any time for me. Honestly, you'd think he was the only parent who had a job. Other kids do sleepovers, but I've never had one before. I really don't ask for much!

So I tried to put my case forward, but he wasn't budging.

'Shanice, I'm sorry, but I don't have the time this weekend for a sleepover party. Maybe in a few months when things are much quieter,' he said.

'Well, first of all, it's not a sleepover party and, secondly, I don't have a few months – Ade has already taken me out shopping with her, and now it's my turn to have her over.'

'Well, that was nice of her, and it will be your turn soon, just not now.'

I sulked all day and night. When it was dinner, I sulked. I sulked at the shop. I sulked for days around the house. If there's one thing my dad doesn't like, it's me sulking. He says it brings the whole house down like a dark cloud looming over us. But I was determined to be miserable and sad. If I bring the mood of the whole house down, then so be it.

Then one day, without warning while I was obviously still sulking, he came into my room and said: 'Okay, Shanice, if we're going to have this sleepover . . .'

Before he could finish, I shrieked, 'WHAT!! YES!'

I leaped off the bed and wrapped my arms round him. 'Thank you, thank you, thank youuuuuuu!!'

'Yes, but on one condition: James is your chaperone, and you have to do exactly as he says – no excuses, no buts, no ifs. He will absolutely be the boss of things.'

'Yeah, for sure. Whatever James says goes,' I said, not meaning a word of it.

James, the boss of me? I tried not to giggle.

I ran downstairs two steps at a time, and called Ade to tell her the good news.

I didn't even say hello. 'SLEEPOVER AT MINE NEXT WEEKEND!' I yelled.

'We love to see it!' Ade yelled back.

'Okay, so bring yourself and your pyjamas – this is going to be so much fun!'

I so wanted my first sleepover to be special. I imagined that Ade had been to a few in her time, but the closest I'd ever got to one was in the movies.

I couldn't get the grin off my face in the week leading up to the sleepover, as I started to plan every detail. What food we'd eat, what activities we would do and, of course, what time we'd go to bed, because I didn't want to fall asleep at, like, 10 p.m. or something – that wouldn't be much of a sleepover, now would it?

On the big day, Dad gave James some money so we could get snacks.

'Have a lovely time!' Dad shouted as we left.

'Trust me, I won't,' James mumbled under his breath. He was only agreeing to chaperone us because he wanted these latest trainers, so overseeing the sleepover was the price he had to pay.

When we got to the shops, it was overwhelming! I wasn't sure what Ade's favourite ice cream was. Was she a chocolate, a strawberry or a vanilla ice-cream girl? I decided to go for strawberry flavour. I love strawberry – I mean, who doesn't? – and it's pink so, yeah, Ade must love it too. I was spending so much time choosing the rest of the snacks that I could tell James was getting impatient. He gives me a particular look when he's annoyed with me. Anyway, in the end, I got everything I needed. We had ice cream, popcorn, pineapple juice, peanut-butter cake swirls and a big chocolate bar each – the limited-edition ones the TV keeps advertising.

By the time Ade arrived, everything was perfect. I had tidied my room and got everything ready. I even sprayed one of Mum's old perfumes around. It smelled like sweet candyfloss.

The bell rang, and when I rushed to open the door Aunty Kim was standing there.

'Hello, Shanice. How are you, darling girl?' she said as she looked right past me at Dad.

She followed up with, 'Hello, Matthew. Just dropping Ade off – she's getting something from the car.' She had a big smile on her face.

Things felt a lil awkward for a few seconds, and then I saw Ade creep up behind her and yell excitedly.

'Heyyy, Shanice!!'

Ade and I couldn't wait to get away from them!

IT WAS THE BEST TWENTY-FOUR HOURS I HAD EVER HAD IN, LIKE, FOREVER!!!

Dad had ordered a DIY pizza kit for us, and we had so much fun making them. I love pineapple and ham on my pizza, but Ade hates that combo. She made a face as I created mine.

'Pineapple doesn't belong on here!' she said. 'I don't understand how you can have it on pizza – it's a fruit!'

Surprisingly, she created a rather boring and bog-standard tomato, cheese and pepperoni pizza.

James had to chaperone us while we made them – as if he can cook or knows what he's doing anyway, but he didn't bother us too much, and spent the whole time on his phone or listening to music.

'Your brother is so quiet,' Ade whispered.

'He makes a lot of noise when he's in his room and when his friends come over. Don't let him fool you.'

We ate our pizzas in front of the TV, which usually I'm never allowed to do, but James said it was okay if we kept the noise down. I guess he is the boss after all!

After we'd cleared up, I showed Ade my room.

'It's never this neat in here – you're getting the red-carpet treatment.'

'Oh wow, your room is so grown-up and pink!' She looked around in awe.

'I don't know if I'd say grown-up, but for my birthday Dad and I redecorated it and ordered some new furniture. If I could stay in here forever, then I would. It's my special place.'

'This is how I'd like my room to be – it's so cool.'

I was secretly gassed that Ade was impressed.

'Guess what I brought for us?' Ade said with a sly smile.

She delved into her little bag and pulled out two pairs of pink pyjamas. I gasped.

'My Aunty Kim got us matching pj's! She's so amazing, isn't she?'

'She really is – this is so sick!'

When I unfolded mine, I saw that they had my name printed on them: SHANICE in fancy white font! It was the best present ever. Do you know how cool that is?

Ade grinned. 'Yeah, she went into town to get them printed. She's taking the "I want to be part of your family" thing really seriously!'

I burst out laughing. 'She sure is! Right, let's change into them and get ready for tonight's activities.'

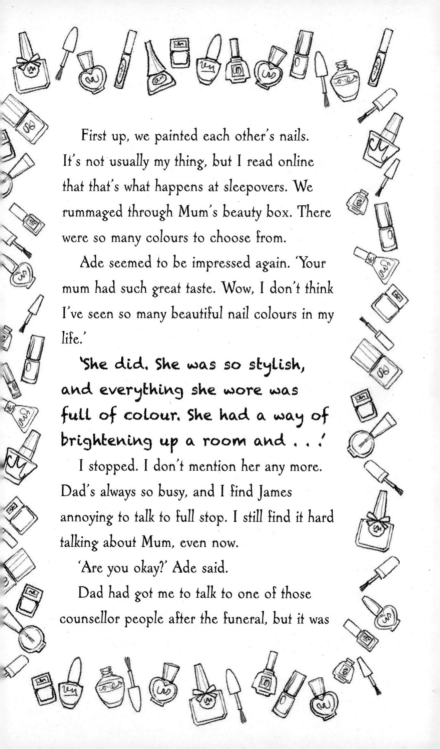

First up, we painted each other's nails.
It's not usually my thing, but I read online
that that's what happens at sleepovers. We
rummaged through Mum's beauty box. There
were so many colours to choose from.

Ade seemed to be impressed again. 'Your
mum had such great taste. Wow, I don't think
I've seen so many beautiful nail colours in my
life.'

**'She did. She was so stylish,
and everything she wore was
full of colour. She had a way of
brightening up a room and . . .'**

I stopped. I don't mention her any more.
Dad's always so busy, and I find James
annoying to talk to full stop. I still find it hard
talking about Mum, even now.

'Are you okay?' Ade said.

Dad had got me to talk to one of those
counsellor people after the funeral, but it was

really hard opening up to them. I dreaded the visits so much, but it was different with Ade. She didn't push me. I could just be myself with her. We spoke about Mum for a lil bit, and I actually felt better. Maybe talking about these things does help after all.

Then we had fun chatting and giggling about the boys in school, Ade has a crush on Kyle Teixeira – he's in Year 9! I guess we were making too much noise, as James interrupted us to say we had to keep it down, and we had two choices. Go to bed or put on a movie. Who does he think he is?

Anyway, we watched a movie – actually, we had a movie marathon. We got through three films! The first was a bit lame – we pretty much chatted through it all. Then Ade wanted a scary film, and it was so terrifying we both had to watch it through parted fingers. As the evening went on, we munched our way through all the snacks.

We had barely slept before it was time to wake up again. I was so tired, I could hardly get out of bed. I needed at least another ten hours of sleep. But it had been so worth it! James begrudgingly made us breakfast. I had orange juice, and Ade had hot chocolate –

another reason why we're the same but different – hot chocolate with breakfast? So not my thing.

When she was leaving, Ade gave me a big hug. She's defo the sister I wish I had.

Not bad for my first sleepover!!

Chapter 17

Ade

Dear Diary,

WHAT A BORING DAY TODAY WAS! Barely even
worth writing about, but it's not like I've got anything
else to do since I've finished all my homework, and
Bisi is hogging the remote . . .

Maths was a drag as usual, as was chemistry,
and I didn't have a single class with Shanice so we
couldn't even have a little gossip or pull faces at
each other across the classroom. I did, however,
have physics again, which was only made less dire
by Amy and Aaliyah — those girls are hilarious! We
spent most of the lesson passing notes about other
people in the class. They were making jokes about

Mrs Buchanan's hair (which does look a little bit like a nest) and how lanky Gemma Osborne is (I'm not being funny but she is!).

Double A can be a bit harsh, but, as they say, they're only being honest, and they never mean anything by it. After class, we walked out together to 8O, but when Shanice saw us her smile changed into a grimace.

'See you at lunch, Ade,' Amy and Aaliyah said in unison.

Shanice had a face like thunder. She wanted me to sit with her at lunch today, but I wanted to hang out with Double A too, so asked her to join us.

'You know I don't like those girls,' she said really quietly. 'And they don't like me.'

'They don't *not* like you,' I said unconvincingly; I knew this wasn't true. 'I think you guys could really get on!'

'I'd rather not. I've already explained why. Can't it just be us?'

I thought about it; I didn't want to leave her

out — she's my best mate. But, for the first few weeks at school, she was the only person I sat with, and I want to make loads of different friends. So I decided to sit with Amy and Aaliyah today.

'I promise I'll walk home with you after school,' I said.

Shanice didn't look very happy and sighed as she walked away. I did feel pretty bad, but surely I'm allowed to have other mates as well? And just because she doesn't like them doesn't mean I can't!

At lunch with Double A, I was a little bit quiet. I scanned the hall, but Shanice was nowhere to be seen. Double A were going on about my birthday plans, as if it was theirs coming up.

'Okay, so we need to work out exactly what you're doing for your birthday, Ade,' said Amy. 'Who's coming, where it's gonna be — we need to start planning! Cinema or restaurant? Or maybe cinema, then restaurant!'

'Um . . . I don't know — maybe both?' I said absent-mindedly.

'What's up with you?' Aaliyah asked, peering at

the phone in her lap.

'Yeah. You're well quiet today,' Amy added.

'I'm all right,' I sighed. 'I just think I might have upset Shanice a bit today because I didn't sit with her at lunch. I wish you guys could be mates — it would make my life a lot easier.'

'Er, never,' Aaliyah said, finally looking up. 'What would make your life easier is if you dropped her altogether. She's a loser.'

'No, she isn't,' I said weakly. 'She's my mate!'

'She doesn't wash!' Amy hit back. 'You wanna be mates with someone who doesn't even change their clothes?'

I felt so silly saying it but I had to. 'Of course she showers,' I said. 'You mean to tell me you guys have never repeated a shirt two days in a row?'

'No,' they said in unison.

'Well, neither have I,' I lied. I'd worn the same shirt several days in a row, but from the look on their faces I knew this was something I could never admit to them. 'But I'm sure plenty of people have, and it doesn't mean they don't shower!'

'Whatever. You have to admit though that she's a

bit of a weirdo. Barely speaks to anyone, always in a strop,' said Amy, nudging me. I shook my head.

'Okay, whatever. If you insist,' Amy said, suddenly bored. 'But she needs to let you have other mates,' she added through a mouthful of pickle-and-ham sandwich. 'Not everyone wants to be a loner like her.'

'Yeah,' Aaliyah said, munching on prawn cocktail crisps. 'She can't force you into being a social reject just because she's one.'

'Come on, guys, she's not a social reject,'
I said quietly.
'She just likes her own company, I think.'

'And that's fine,' said Aaliyah. 'But it's not fine when it means she's your only company.'

At that moment, the bell rang, thank God. I felt guilty just listening to them.

'Come on, girls,' Amy said, dusting crisps off her lap as she stood up. 'I forgot my PE kit so I need to speak to Mr Oppong before next period.'

As Aaliyah and I got up too, I saw Amy's face screw up. 'Urgh, what's that?'

I was immediately mortified — my diary was halfway out of my backpack. I tried to stuff it back in, but Amy was already attempting to prise it open.

'Oh my gosh, I recognise this!' she squealed. 'Shanice has one of these. Is this hers??'

'Of course it is!' Aaliyah cut in before I had time to respond. 'As if Ade would sit around writing about her feelings all day, like some oversensitive weirdo. Right, Ade?'

'Duh,' I said without thinking. It just came out, I swear. 'Who do you guys think I am?'

I don't even know why I said it, but once I had it was too late. I felt bad, but also relieved, to be completely honest. They'd have probably made me feel worse if I'd admitted it was mine, right?

After school, Shanice still seemed to be in a bit of a sulk.

'Please don't be annoyed at me,' I said, pulling my best apologetic face. 'I just wanted to spend one lunchtime with Double A, that's all! I'm new here, remember?'

Shanice sighed. 'All right,' she said. 'I get it. I know you guys have got close, so you're gonna hang out. I expected it on some level. Let's just stop talking about them, okay?'

I nodded. I didn't like it when she spoke about them, or when they spoke about her. It was always so awkward! I know they'll never get on, but I do hope that doesn't get in the way of either friendship . . .

Chapter 18

Shanice

Hey,

Feeling a little down today. Let me tell you why . . .

So we've been back at Archbishop Academy for a few weeks now, and I guess things are ticking along like they usually do. Year 8 is a little more intense than Year 7, but overall it's more of the same. I sometimes still get lost in the corridors, which means I've been late to lessons a few times. Mr Oppong threatened me with detention the other day, which was bang out of order because it's not like I'm the only one. He picks on me for no reason, I swear. But today we had this thing where, as well as having to actually go to lessons, the teachers insist on making us school ambassadors or receptionists. It's all part of a scheme to teach us 'skills useful for your lives beyond our time at school'.

Surprise, surprise, I didn't want to be an ambassador for any school, especially not for one I don't like. Anyway, parents were all sent emails about it, which meant that Dad was breathing down my neck this morning.

He knew this was my worst nightmare, and I was totally out of my comfort zone.

'Cheer up, Shanice – you might actually enjoy it.'

He continued reading the email out word for word. How the scheme is a 'unique opportunity to learn more about how the school functions'.

What a lie. It's gonna be us kids doing the work adults in the school can't be bothered to do – half a day per term where we get dumped with a load of tasks. What happened to just going to school for an education? Now they're training us to learn skills we don't want or need! I much preferred the days in primary school when they sent us home with a letter instead. Back then, I could at least have thrown away the letter and then conveniently been off sick.

I already knew it was going to be a really annoying day. I had to play receptionist and spend a whole morning working with Chante, my partner. She's a nice girl and very quiet, but it was a very FULL-ON morning: we had to take urgent messages to students, collect and check registers, do lesson checks, collect work for students who were not in their usual lessons and meet and greet visitors to the school. It was very tiring. Tiring and boring. Why this is anyone's job in real life, I do not know. Chante seemed to love it though, and all the teachers seemed to love her loving it. She's not exactly a suck-up in the traditional sense, like a teacher's pet, but how on earth could she enjoy it??? Like I said, she's nice but definitely a bit odd.

Afterwards, we had to write about what we'd learned and enjoyed about the experience. Ugh, I didn't enjoy any of it, and now I have to waste time lying that I did. In the end, I copied Chante word for word, which she didn't seem to mind at all:

I really enjoyed today because I was able to learn so much about Archbishop Academy and about time management, helping others and having to be professional.

A bunch of lies. I was so looking forward to escaping and moaning to Ade. But, when I went to find her at our usual spot outside the cafeteria at lunchtime, she was nowhere to be seen. I waited for such ages that I was in danger of missing lunch altogether.

Where could she be? Maybe she got detention? Or she felt ill and was sent home? At this rate, she could have been abducted by aliens because there was no sign of her anywhere.

Mrs P walked by just as I was starting to get really worried.

'What are you doing out here on your lonesome, darling? Haven't you had lunch yet?'

'I'm waiting for Ade. I think something's happened – we usually meet here for lunch, but she's gone AWOL,' I said, looking around.

'Ade? She's already in the cafeteria, love,' Mrs P said, puzzled.

'Already?' Now I looked puzzled.

'You poor thing, have you been waiting all this time?'
she said.

'Yeah, pretty much. She said this morning that we'd
catch up over lunch, so I've been waiting for her.'

'Well, the dinner staff are five minutes away from
packing up. I'd go in now if I were you,' she said.

I wasn't hungry any more.

I just had a massive knot in my stomach.

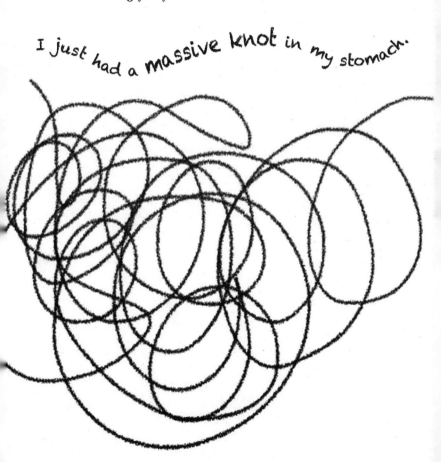

When I walked in, there she was . . . sitting with the Double-A girls, giggling. They're always sniggering, probably at someone else's expense. Maybe mine? My heart sank. So she basically blew me off again to sit with them. That's the second time she's done it this week. We made eye contact briefly, and it was a lil awkward. She smiled, and I smiled back. I tried not to look upset. She'd probably forgotten that we were meant to sit together today.

But I couldn't face lunch in the end, and usually I love spag-bol Thursdays. Even the triple portion of cheese couldn't tempt me.

I was beginning to have a bad feeling about our friendship. Not because of Ade, she's lovely – she's literally my best mate. But it's just my luck that those girls have got their claws into her too and so quickly. Couldn't they have given me a year with my best friend before interfering? I don't want to blame Ade – I know it must be hard starting a new school and trying to fit in with people – but she has me. Am I not enough for her?

Anyway, I can only imagine how hard it is to juggle those horrible girls. I just really hope this doesn't affect our friendship too much. Ade is new, and she probably hasn't realised how dreadful the Double As are. I don't want to make today a big deal so I won't mention it. It's not the first time I've spent lunchtime alone in this school – nothing new there. I just have to try and get over what happened today.

CHAPTER 19
 CHATBACK

@PrincessSuperAde: You seen my latest pic on ChatBack?

> **@_Shannyxo:** Yeah, it's cool. I already liked it.

@PrincessSuperAde: Oh no, I must have missed it among the sea of likes I got :P

> **@_Shannyxo:** Loool probably.

@PrincessSuperAde: Double A helped me get my hair like that. Took so many hairbands!

@_Shannyxo: Personally I liked your hair better before though. It was more . . . you.

@PrincessSuperAde: Well, ChatBack doesn't agree with you! I've never had more likes! Definitely think it makes me look older. It's just unreal.

@_Shannyxo: 'Unreal?' You sound like Amy and Aaliyah!

@PrincessSuperAde: Lol, no, I don't! And if I did is that such a bad thing?

@_Shannyxo: Yes . . .

@PrincessSuperAde: Why?

@_Shannyxo: Because you should sound like yourself! Be yourself!

@PrincessSuperAde: You just don't like Amy! Or Aaliyah :(

@_Shannyxo: I don't lol.

@PrincessSuperAde: See! Honestly, if you got to know them, I reckon you'd really get on.

@_Shannyxo: I've known them longer than you lol. Trust me, they're bad news. And they're not going to like the fact we're friends, you'll see.

@PrincessSuperAde: Come on, don't be paranoid. I know you guys aren't friends but there's no reason we wouldn't be!

@_Shannyxo: I know you think I'm worried just because I don't like them, but it's not just about them. It's about you too. I don't want things to change. I don't want you to change.

@PrincessSuperAde: Why would I change? Come on, Shanice, you're overthinking things as usual . . .

@_Shannyxo: Lol, you might be right, always in my head. But still. Just promise me we'll remain mates, yeah?

@PrincessSuperAde: Well, duh, of course!

                                @_Shannyxo: Best mates?

@PrincessSuperAde: Yessss, best mates <3! Why wouldn't we? Now stop being a weirdo lol.

Chapter 20
Shanice

Heyyy,

It's the weekend! No homework, no teachers. I don't even have to go to Dad's shop today – James is staying in, and so Dad says I can too. Yay! I'm not to bother James because he's studying for his upcoming exams. That's totally fine with me – the less I see of him the better.

The sun woke me up like it always does, but today the way it was streaming in made me think of Mum as she ~~loves~~ loved the sun. On days like this, it defo feels as if she's shining down on me.

The first anniversary of Mum's passing is coming up. I never like saying the horrible 'd' word. Mum was ill for a long time, so her passing didn't necessarily come as a surprise to us. I wish that could have made things easier, but it really didn't. It was still the hardest thing in the world when the time did come. I don't even think I'll ever find the words to describe how sad it made me feel.

I overheard one of the aunties at her funeral saying how she was worried that, because I was so young, it would be harder for me to remember Mum. I was so angry at her for suggesting that my mum was so easily forgettable! **My biggest fear is losing those memories. I mean, I couldn't, could I? How can you forget the most important person in your life???** I made a promise to myself that I wouldn't ever lose a single memory of her – from the little ones to the big ones.

It'll almost be a year soon, so I wanted to do something special for the anniversary. I spoke to Mrs P about it after English on Friday. Mrs P is one of those people who gets me more than most.

'Even though loss is out of our control, making

143

positive memories, so that family and friends aren't forgotten, is within our control,' she said.

'But how do I do that?'

'Why don't you create a special book or photo album? Also, you love writing. You could write down your favourite stories and memories of her, even a poem or two. Your book could be full of things that will help tell the story of who your mum was.'

'That is such a cool idea, Mrs P.'

I had so many ideas for my special book. I could include Mum's favourite food, her favourite colours, our holidays!

After school, I went to the local arts-and-crafts shop and used some of my pocket money to buy a large scrapbook of thick cardstock. It was sturdy and plain with an interior spiral binding. It was perfect.

I started to rummage through all our old photo albums on Saturday morning. So many baby pics of James and photos of Mum and Dad. Not nearly as many of me! Dad had to explain to me that, when James was born, it wasn't so easy to store pictures digitally, and he had to print out photos – so old-fashioned!

James walked in on me sitting at the kitchen table,

going through the albums.

'What are you doing with my pictures?' he said suspiciously.

'They're not all of you actually,' I declared loudly.

'Then what are you doing? Don't do anything that's going to make Dad angry when he gets back because you know I'll get the blame.'

'The world doesn't revolve round you, James. There's more to life,' I said with as much sarcasm as I could muster.

I just wanted to be alone! Urghhhh.

'I'm not looking for a babysitter, James. You can leave.'

He sat down anyway and started flicking through one of the albums.

I looked at him. Why wouldn't he just go? He must have been very bored of revising.

'Last time I checked, this was my house too, and I can sit anywhere I want to,' he said with a patronising smile.

'Well, if you must know, I'm creating a special book for Mum. Mrs P says it'll help me hold on to my memories of her as I grow up.'

I didn't think he was listening – he was just staring at one of the pictures – but he had been.

'I have a playlist that I made to remember her.'

'Ohhh.'

'Yeah, Mum was really into music when she was my age. She was gonna be a DJ at some point. She used to sneak off to all these underground raves and gigs. Yeah, so it's how I remember her, by listening to the music she loved. It does help.'

First of all, who knew James could string two sentences together, and, second of all, who knew he was . . . well, I don't know how to word it . . . I mean . . . a little bit normal and had feelings and stuff?

'I'm trying to create my own memories, but I can't find nearly as many photos of me as there are of you. It's not fair!'

'Just use the cloud software to download them.'

'But I don't have access to that.'

'Hmm, okay, well, I do . . . I have the password, but don't tell Dad I gave it to you.'

He went upstairs, brought back his laptop and, within a few clicks, had opened this thing called Buzzcloud.

And there they were. Hundreds and hundreds of

photos started to load on to the screen . . . pictures of me, pictures of us smiling. Dad with actual hair, wow. Can't remember that! Mum with her usual coloured braids and her stylish outfits.

I looked at James as he was scrolling, and I gave him a hug.

'What's that for?' he said jokingly, but with a smile.

'Nothing.'

Urgh, that will defo be the last hug I'll ever be giving my brother.

So that's what we did all afternoon. Sitting in Dad's office together, we printed out all the pictures I wanted.

These were memories I'd cherish for life, and for some bizarre reason I knew I'd cherish that afternoon with James too. We don't have many of these moments, but I know deep down that I love James very much – he reminds me of Mum.

Chapter 21

Ade

Dear Diary,

GOSH, TODAY WAS *SOOO* AWKWARD. Where do I start? I guess from the beginning would be best...

The day actually started off quite good — that's the thing. Last night, Amy and Aaliyah told me how they'd be doing their hair so we could all have matching styles, and I'd be lying if I said I wasn't excited. I met them at the bus stop, and they both gave a big Double-A thumbs up to my do, which was great, and then we walked into school together. (I told Shanice I was running late and to go ahead without me, which was true, but only because I was hanging back so I could walk in with Double A.)

As we went in, I debuted my topknot alongside Amy and Aaliyah (mine was a big Afro puff on the top of my head, hair slicked back courtesy of lots of Bisi's hair gel), and everyone's heads turned. The whole class was going on about how unreal we looked — I can't wait to upload today's look to ChatBack!

Shanice, of course, was less impressed. She pulled a face when I walked in with them, and even though she didn't say anything I could practically hear her moaning. She is my best mate obviously, but I have to admit that sometimes she can be a bit needy!!

In class, Amy and Aaliyah went to sit in their usual spot and ushered me over to an empty seat beside them. (I think Lakshmi Murthy had sat there before. I wonder how they got her to move?) I could see Shanice out of the corner of my eye as I sat down with them. I've already tried loads of times to involve her, but she's made it clear that she doesn't want to hang around with them.

When the bell rang, I went over to say hey quickly before I headed to maths, and she gave a forced smile — at least it was a smile though. And I made sure I sat with her at lunch because I knew she'd have had a massive sulk if I didn't, but how am I supposed to make other friends if she wants me all to herself?

'Are you all right?' she asked when I was being a bit quiet at the lunch table.

'Yeah,' I replied with a mouthful of chips, hoping

she wouldn't push. She did though, as always.

'Are you sure? You just seem a bit off today.'

I caught a glimpse of the Double As giggling at the phone in Aaliyah's lap. I felt a pang of something, I'm not sure what — jealousy that they were having fun without me? Irritation that I wasn't sitting with them and was stuck with Shanice instead? I really do like her, but she's not the only friend I want to have at Archbishop Academy.

'Shanice, I'm fine! Gosh!'

After lunch, we had English, and that's where the problems began. We're doing this really interesting book called *Jane Eyre* — it was written all the way back in **1847**! Things were so different back then that Charlotte Brontë, the author, had to release it under a man's name so it would be taken seriously — she published it under the name Currer Bell. When people realised she might be a woman, she started getting rubbish reviews — how crazy is that?

I thought it was going to be a boring and dry read, but it was kinda great! I hope I get an A for my homework on this book. Jane is a bit of an outcast, sort of in her own little world, and reminds me a bit of Shanice at times.

Anyway, English is technically my favourite subject, but not my favourite class. Mrs P is always there, lurking, finding something to moan about. Plus, it always gets really awkward with Shanice and the Double As: juggling best friends is no easy feat and today was no exception. In fact, today was particularly bad.

'Okay, everyone,' said Mrs Adams with a clap that cut through the class's afternoon chatter. 'Get into groups of three to brainstorm the themes of money and class in *Jane Eyre* so far. You'll present your findings back to everyone afterwards.'

As soon as she said it, my face felt hot. I saw Shanice smiling expectantly, and Amy and Aaliyah beckoning me over, the friendship bracelets jangling on their wrists. I wanted one badly.

'Coming, girls!' I said and mouthed 'sorry' to Shanice.

And I really was sorry — she looked so let down. I wished I could split myself in two and hang out with all of them at once, but I'll make it up to Shanice tonight on ChatBack and then again tomorrow, definitely. And next time we have to work in groups I'll do it with her. I did feel pretty bad — but Amy and Aaliyah are my friends too. And it's not like Jacob Owens and Carl Turner (she was automatically paired with them because no one else chose her) are all that bad . . . But she did cut a lonely figure, sitting between them as they chatted away over her head.

I pulled up a chair next to Amy and Aaliyah. Their smiles almost looked a bit smug, and I felt a pang of guilt again — they knew I'd choose them over Shanice.

'You sat with Powers at lunchtime,' Aaliyah said. 'I can smell it!'

I said nothing. We didn't do much in our group — we spent most of the time yakking about ChatBack and Kyle Teixeira (he's cut his hair and looks so unreal!) — so, when it came to our presentation, it wasn't the strongest. I was the only one who'd done the reading so had pretty much written the brainstorm single-handedly. When we went up to the front, we were just winging it — it was the longest two minutes ever!

'Please concentrate next time, girls,' Mrs Adams said through pursed lips. As we sat down, giggling, I saw Mrs P out of the corner of my eye giving us daggers.

Next up were Jacob, Carl and Shanice. She didn't say a word as the boys gave their feedback — she was looking down at her shoes almost the whole time. Double A were whispering and giggling throughout the presentation. Shanice didn't react at first, but I'm sure she could hear them. Then, after a while, I heard her mutter 'idiots' under her breath. They started to giggle harder. I wondered what they were laughing at, but didn't want to ask. If I ignored them, it wasn't me doing or saying anything nasty. But I could see Amy wafting her hand through the air and Aaliyah pinching her nose, making a gagging sound.

When Shanice's group had finished, she sat down, and for the rest of the lesson she didn't look at me once. But I can't say I was too worried about it — we'd sort it out later. Meanwhile, Amy, Aaliyah and I had a blast, gossiping about people in our year and planning our posts for ChatBack.

'Girls, be quiet,' Mrs P said, placing her fingers to her lips.

She must have shushed us at least four more times, but before we knew it the bell had gone. We could barely hear her over the noise of chairs scraping the floor, pencil cases being thrown in bags and Year 8s chattering away. Mrs Adams shook her head as she sat down to file her papers. Shanice had bolted before I even had the chance to catch up with her and, as Aaliyah, Amy and I were walking out of the door into the hallway, I felt a tap on my shoulder. It was Mrs P.

'Ade,' she said. 'Can I have a word?'

'Oooh, Ade's in trouble!' Amy and Aaliyah said at the same time. But what had I done that they hadn't? All three of us were being silly in the lesson.

I followed Mrs P into a corner by a set of lockers, flicking through a set of ready-made excuses.

'Yes, miss?' I said, chewing the inside of my cheek.

'I hope I haven't alarmed you,' she said with furrowed brows. 'Just thought I'd check in.'

I was definitely alarmed. Mrs P only seems to notice me when she has something to complain about.

'I just wanted to have a quick chat with you about something.'

'. . . Okay?'

'Well, someone. Shanice.'

'Shanice?' I wasn't alarmed now, just confused. 'What about her?'

'Well, I do hope you don't mind me getting involved.' She looked around to ensure no one was listening. 'But she doesn't seem to be her usual self. She's always been quiet, but now she appears to be going even further into her shell. Am I right in thinking that you girls were quite close when you first started here?'

'. . . Yeah?'

'You seemed to get on very well. Like a house on fire. She was the most bubbly I'd seen her at Archbishop when you came along.'

I shifted on the spot uncomfortably.

'But it appears you've drifted apart recently.'

'That's not true!' I said defensively. 'I speak to her all the time on ChatBack. It's not like we're not friends any more.'

Mrs P pursed her lips. 'I understand. But sometimes people need a friend offline too.' She sighed. 'Shanice is a bit shy. She's quite quiet and doesn't make friends easily. I don't mean to overstep the line or interfere, but I know she appreciates your friendship. And I am slightly worried by how isolated she's become over the last few weeks. It's great that you've made lots of new friends since you've been here, but I do hope Shanice isn't being left out. Thanks for the chat, Ade.'

And, just like that, she was gone. After saying she didn't want to interfere, after hop, skipping and jumping over whatever line, she just disappeared.

I was mortified — Mrs P had basically told me I was being a bad mate to Shanice — was that even allowed? I hurried along the corridor to catch up with Amy and Aaliyah, spotting their ponytails swinging back and forth as they walked.

'What did she want?' asked Amy.

I lied through my teeth. 'Oh, er, she said she wanted to check some of my answers to last week's homework. She wasn't too impressed with it.'

'Surprise, surprise,' Aaliyah tutted. 'She's always got something to moan about. You better watch out — she's gonna be picking on you even more now you're part of our gang.'

'Part of your gang?' I repeated with a grin, practically forgetting everything Mrs P and I had talked about. I tried to play it cool, but it was no use.

'Well, obviously!' Aaliyah said, hitting me in the shoulder. 'Isn't she, Amy?'

'You're definitely part of our gang,' Amy said, nodding. 'In fact, we have to be the Triple As now, since there's three of us.'

'YES!' Aaliyah said, stopping to jump up and down on the spot.

'We are the **TRIPLE-A girls.**
Three is the magic number.
You should totally change your name on ChatBack!'

The Triple As. It just sounds right, has a ring to it. I'm a Triple-A girl now! Definitely changing my screen name as soon as I get on ChatBack. I wonder if they'll get me a friendship bracelet too? It is my birthday soon . . .

After school, going to the park with Amy and Aaliyah nearly made up for everything that had happened earlier. They taught me this sick new dance challenge, which is super hard and super fast. They got it so easily — but I managed to keep up, and it looked amazing!

'Ade, you're an unreal dancer!' Aaliyah told me afterwards. 'We're gonna break the internet!'

We're uploading it tonight — I just know we're going to get tons of likes.

Today was weird and really awkward, but I'm not going to let Mrs P — or Shanice for that matter — make me feel bad for having other mates. I'll catch up with Shanice tonight — hope she's not going to be in a mood.

Chapter 22
Shanice

Heyyyy,

I've got so much homework to do so I can't even write for long. I know, right? Very annoying. I have maths and science due tomorrow. So unfair. I feel overwhelmed by it all!

Remember what I was saying about Year 8 not being much more intense than Year 7? Scrap that. It's proving to be *soooooo* much more intense, with a capital I, and I'm not just talking about the homework or teachers who can be a real pain. I'm talking about friend stuff too. It was much easier when I didn't even have a best friend because now it's hard to know if I'm coming or going with Ade any more. Are we still best friends or just fake best friends? She's become so on/off with me. At first, I thought it was just the Double-A girls getting their claws into her, but now I worry that Ade likes the whole popularity thing at Archbishop Academy far too much!

I think my dad's noticed something because I've stopped talking about her as much at home. But her birthday's coming up so tonight, at dinner, I asked if we could get Ade a present, and he looked surprised and half jokingly said: 'I didn't think you two were still best friends. I sensed some distance.'

'We are still friends, but things are a little bit different these days . . .'

He smiled encouragingly, but I just stared at my plate. He just wouldn't get it, so why bother?

But he wouldn't let it go. 'Shanice, different doesn't always mean bad – I bet she's still very fond of you and loves being your friend. She's probably still finding her feet at school. You've been there for a whole year longer than her, remember?'

'That's not the issue—' By this point, I had a little lump in my throat.

'Friendship is a two-way street. You can't force anyone to be friends with you – it has to feel natural and—'

It was my turn to cut him off.

'I wasn't forcing her. I mean I'm not forcing her,' I said defensively.

'I know. What I mean is that all relationships, even friendships, need a little tender loving care every bit as much as a flower in the garden needs water.'

'Sure.' I rolled my eyes.

Tender loving care. It's not that deep, is it? We're not in a relationship.

Friendship was so much easier at nursery.

Maybe I'm just overthinking it – all I know is that on the outside Ade is a great best friend. She makes me laugh, and when we spend time together I feel good. When good things happen, she's the first one I want to tell, and even when bad things happen she's also the first one I want to turn to. As I said, it's her birthday soon, so I really hope we'll be able to spend some time together and get back to hanging out like we used to do. I have an idea for a present, and I hope she loves it!

Anyway, back to this boring maths homework – I really couldn't care less about fractions, percentages, ratio and proportions . . . urgh.

CHAPTER 23
CHATBACK

@TripleAde: Hey :) You all right?

> **@_Shannyxo:** Hey . . . Didn't really see you much at school today. Again :(

@TripleAde: I'm sorry :(You know how Amy and Aaliyah are. They can be a bit, you know.

> **@_Shannyxo:** Hm. You've changed your screen name.

@TripleAde: What was your first clue? Lol, no duh, I'm a Triple A-girl, so have to represent :') #Unreal

@_Shannyxo: Hmmm . . .

@TripleAde: What, you don't like?

@_Shannyxo: I just don't get why you had to change it is all. It was fine the way it was.

@TripleAde: @PrincessSuperAde was babyish. What am I, a Year 7?

@_Shannyxo: No, you're Ade. Princess Super Ade.

@TripleAde: It's just a kiddie nickname my dad, who doesn't even bother to see me, gave me years ago. Things change.

@_Shannyxo: They really do.

@TripleAde: What's that supposed to mean?

@_Shannyxo: Sigh, nothing.

@TripleAde: Don't be like that.

@_Shannyxo: I'm not being like anything.

@TripleAde: You are. I can tell from the tone of your messages.

@_Shannyxo: This is how I always type lol. You're the one with all the caps locks and emojis, remember?

@TripleAde: Looool, true that :P

@_Shannyxo: Exactly! Anyway, I've been meaning to ask you – what do you want for your bday next week? I'm rubbish at picking presents.

@TripleAde: That's a good question! You know what, anything edible usually works for me lol.

@_Shannyxo: Lol, okay, noted! Have you decided how you're celebrating?

@TripleAde: Um not yet, still not sure if I can be bothered to do anything for it lol.

@_Shannyxo: Really? I thought for sure you'd want to do something! Bowling or cinema or ice-skating or something!

@TripleAde: I'm just not sure if I can be bothered this year . . . We'll see.

@_Shannyxo: Okay, well, if you need any ideas or help with anything, you know where I am. ChatBack, the only place where I seem to exist to you . . .

@_Shannyxo: I'm joking btw lol.

@TripleAde: Haha lol, yeah yeah. But thanks, I'll let you know x

Chapter 24
Shanice

Hey,

I have some bad news. I'm not getting the bearded dragon after all. Well, I mean it's been weeks now and she's nowhere to be seen. I'm so annoyed. It's actually very unfair. I've become so responsible at home recently. I tidy my room without being asked, I load the dishwasher after dinner, I water the plants in the front room AND I don't fight with James as much as much any more! What else does Dad want from me??? Like I'm really trying here. I must be the most responsible thirteen-year-old in this town. And what do I get to show for it? *Nothinggggg.*

Anyway, today is Ade's thirteenth birthday, whoop, whoop. I'm so surprised she decided not to celebrate it properly in the end. I thought she would have had a lil party or gone bowling. It took me ages to decide what present to get for her. I really hope she likes it. I've tried not to dwell on the fact that I feel I only exist to Ade online over the last few weeks. ChatBack is, like, the worst. It feels as though Archbishop Academy runs on it these days – everyone congregates there after school – it's becoming the place to be seen. Seen acting like a fool if you ask me.

When we're in school, Ade spends the majority of her time with the Double-A girls. **They're now calling themselves the Triple-A girls. They stomp around the school like they own it.** I don't think they know how ridiculous they look with their hair all done up the same and their matching outfits. They're going for that girl-band look, but end up looking like they're three little clones!

That's the thing about feelings. I overanalyse things and focus on all the ways life can go wrong, and then

I just think the worst of people. My dad says it's a coping mechanism, and it's because, deep down, no one likes being rejected. He says adults go through the same thing. He sure is right. I guess if I say I don't like anyone, then, if they say they don't like me, it doesn't hurt as much. Maybe that's why I've been so OTT with Ade - because she's the first person I can say I've liked at school. Anyway, I don't want to lose her now, do I? Especially to something and people so SILLY.

I've got to write this birthday card to Ade - so Dad can drop it off at hers on his way to the shop this morning.

Peace out, babes!

Ade

Dear Diary,

HAPPY BIRTHDAY TO ME! At long last, I'm thirteen years old! Though you'd think I was still seven if Mum's present is anything to go by: she got me a Doodle Pillowcase for my birthday. Who am I, Funmi? Speaking of Funmi, she and Bisi did all right with their gifts this year. Funmi gave me a string of LED fairy lights, and I got a really nice vanilla-and-cherry-flavoured body mist spray from Bisi.

'Hopefully, this means you'll stop stealing my perfume,' Bisi said, eyebrow raised as she handed it over. I laughed nervously — that girl has CCTV in her bedroom, I swear!

I got a gift from *him* too — a pair of brand-new headphones.

'Isn't that so kind of him?' my mum cooed as he handed it over smugly.

'Thanks,' I mumbled reluctantly.

I ran off, to get away from him before he tried to start up a conversation, but also because I needed to check the post. A card from Grandma and Grandad, one from Aunty Kim with a tenner slipped in it — she really is the best. I kept looking and looking, but there was nothing from Dad. I don't even know why I bother, and I won't be bothering again. I'm thirteen now, and I can already feel myself getting wiser, more mature. Dad is never gonna send me a card again, and me searching the post every birthday, checking my phone for messages that won't come, isn't going to change that.

I had another realisation today too. You know how I've been struggling to keep my friendship with Shanice on track offline, and that she feels I only talk to her on ChatBack these days? I've flat-out denied it and argued with her about it for ages now. But guess what? Maybe she's right and has a point.

Think about it. I'm part of Triple A now — Amy and Aaliyah officially said it themselves — and naturally that means I'm gonna be seeing a lot more of them and a bit less of Shanice. Only at school though — it's not like we don't talk any more. We're still mates, and we still talk all the time . . . on ChatBack. But who says a friendship that takes place primarily on social media isn't a real one? It's where most people chat these days, isn't it?

So, with that in mind, I've made a decision. One that I'm still a tiny bit uneasy about (though Amy and Aaliyah think it's a great idea). I'd been wondering what to do for my birthday that will work for everyone involved, and so far I've been stumped. The problem is that Shanice doesn't get on with Amy and Aaliyah and most of the other Year 8 girls that we hang out with after school. And, as that's most of the people I want to invite to my birthday party, it's going to make things really difficult. In fact, Shanice is kind of the issue here.

'If you're going to be part of our gang, you need to make some choices,' Aaliyah said, playing with the end of her chunky black French braid. 'It's like how you started dressing better once we all started hanging out together. And became way more popular. Things have to change for things to change, you know?'

Amy nodded furiously, the end of her own French braid bobbing up and down behind her. 'Aaliyah's right,' she said. 'You've got to be more careful who you hang out with. Like I know Shanice is your mate and everything, but she doesn't really fit in with, well . . . anyone. I'm not sure how having her —' she waved her right hand in a circular motion — 'in our space really works.'

'Exactly!' Aaliyah said. 'She's not very **triple A,** and you're part of that now, so . . . **it doesn't really work, does it?'**

'She doesn't have to be Triple A though, does she?' I said with a shrug. 'You guys don't have to talk to her just because I do.'

'Yeah, but your birthday, Ade,' Amy insisted. 'It's

supposed to be fun and have all the best people from our year, everyone we get along with. And then there's going to be Shanice Powers, sat in the corner like a bad smell . . . literally.'

Aaliyah held her nose. 'Maybe it's best if she doesn't come?'

So today I decided on the cinema, followed by this fifties-style milkshake-and-burger restaurant that opened last week in the shopping centre to celebrate my thirteenth birthday. And I also decided not to invite Shanice. I know it sounds bad, but I can't make her fit in with everyone else and can't force them to get on with her. Maybe keeping the friendships separate isn't such a bad thing. No awkwardness, no misunderstandings.

I accidentally let it slip to my mum though when she asked if Shanice and I wanted a lift to the restaurant, and she hit the roof.

'This is how you repay her? After everything she's done to welcome you to that school of yours? Have you girls fallen out? What happened?'

I shook my head and opened my mouth to explain,

but she was off again. 'And to think she was the first friend you made, and now you've turned your back on her like everyone else. You said she had a hard time at Archbishop, and now you want to contribute to it? All because you have newer, more popular friends? You think I haven't seen you changing how you talk and dress these past few weeks, to fit in with those other girls? I never had you down as a sheep. Adesola, I am not happy about this.'

I only get the full-name treatment when she's really angry with me — or disappointed. She went on and on at me — on my birthday! About *my* birthday! She even rang Aunty Kim about it, livid.

'Can you believe it?' I overheard her saying from the living room. 'The only friend she had when she first got here, she's now abandoned. I know! Maybe you can talk some sense into her.'

As soon as I heard her say those words, I legged it to the bus stop. It was already bad enough that Mum was having a go at me — but nobody knows how to make me feel bad like Aunty Kim does. Her disappointment hit twice as hard.

When I got to the cinema, it took me a minute

to spot my birthday group. I couldn't see Amy and Aaliyah in the foyer and, though I spotted lots of girls around my age chattering away as they queued for popcorn, I didn't immediately recognise anyone. I'd invited six other girls from our year — not people I'm close to or anything, but Amy and Aaliyah think they're cool, so it's fine. They all get on, laugh at the same things, like the same stuff, and fancy Kyle Teixeira. There's no awkwardness or friction. No big differences that make anyone else uncomfortable.

'Ade!' I turned round and there were Amy and Aaliyah, in matching blue dresses with their hair down and straightened.

'Happy birthday!'

they said in singsong voices.

Amy passed me a small red box with a bow on top and grinned. 'Open it.'

I did so hurriedly, and inside was a braided friendship bracelet with a gold A pendant.

'In pink, just for you,' smiled Aaliyah.

I hugged them both tightly. 'I love it! It's unreal!' I was already technically an official Triple-A girl, but this made it even *more* official.

We then saw some superhero movie (I say saw — most of us just chatted our way through it, to be honest). I can barely remember what happened — and then went on to the restaurant, where we ate our body weight in burgers and hot dogs, washed down with fizzy drinks and milkshakes. Then the waiter came over with a huge chocolate birthday cake, and the whole restaurant joined in to sing to me as I blew out my candles.

It was a pretty epic day — I have to admit I did miss Shanice though. I missed our private jokes. She's a fan of superhero movies — she would have been able to explain what on earth was happening. And she loves a good burger. What is she going to say when she realises she wasn't invited to my birthday celebration? I am dreading that conversation. But hey — at least there was no weirdness today.

When I got home, I noticed a parcel on the doorstep — another present! I tucked it under my arm as I made my way indoors and checked my phone. Everyone was posting cool pictures from today on ChatBack.

As soon as I got to my room (avoiding Mum as best as I could), I opened the red box from Amy and Aaliyah to admire my new bracelet. I snapped a picture and posted it on ChatBack before I even wore it — and the likes just wouldn't stop. I don't want to jinx it, but I think I might hit 500!

When I scrolled down ChatBack, I saw Amy and Aaliyah had posted the group photo with us all sticking our tongues out.

But my mouth dropped open when I realised they'd tagged Shanice in it, even though **she hadn't been there!**

That was unnecessarily mean. Why do they do things like that? Shanice never starts anything with them. She's going to be so upset when she sees this. I just have to hope it was an accident, though I'm pretty sure it wasn't . . .

To make matters worse, when I read the card attached to the parcel, I saw it was from Shanice. She'd bought me a really lovely spa kit — must have cost her a fortune, probably all her pocket money. So much for no awkwardness today — I feel more than awkward. I feel terrible! I need to speak to her as soon as I can. I hope she sees where I'm coming from. Sometimes I'm not sure I do . . .

Chapter 26
Shanice

Wow. *Wow.* *Wow.*

Where do I even begin?

So Ade actually had a birthday thing and didn't even invite me. Then I was tagged in a picture on ChatBack of her having a great time with those girls (I can't bear to write their names in my journal ever again!!) that I had obviously deliberately been left out of. I can't even articulate how I feel currently. Do I feel angry?

Upset? Hurt? Probably a mixture of all three. I feel so disappointed in Ade. What did I do to deserve this? She was meant to be my best friend and have my back. I don't think I've ever felt so hurt and sad before.

Sorry, G2G. I'm gonna just watch some TV to take my mind off this.

CHAPTER 27
∎
CHATBACK

@TripleAde: Hey. Thanks for the birthday gift. It's actually the best present I got this year. Maybe any year.

@_Shannyxo: Hey. Happy birthday. You're welcome.

@TripleAde: I understand you must be annoyed with me.

@_Shannyxo: Not annoyed. I'm hurt. You told me you weren't doing anything for your birthday, Ade. Why lie?

@TripleAde: I know. I'm sorry. I wasn't sure what I was doing at that point and just wanted to make sure whatever I did wasn't awkward . . .

@_Shannyxo: And how's that working out for you?

@TripleAde: Not great tbh. I didn't think. Or I thought too much and now I've hurt you. That genuinely wasn't what I wanted.

@_Shannyxo: Well, it's what's happened. Amy and Aaliyah are so spiteful too. They tagged me in the picture just to upset me. I can't believe you'd rather not invite me to avoid falling out with girls like that. I guess falling out with me doesn't matter at all, huh?

@TripleAde: It's not that, I swear. It's just . . . well, you'd be the first to admit you don't get on with them or most other people at Archbishop. I did plan on us celebrating separately.

@_Shannyxo: You don't even talk to most of the girls you were out with! They're Amy and Aaliyah's mates, not yours! You sold me out for mean girls and strangers!

@TripleAde: I'm sorry! I am genuinely sorry, okay? I should have thought it through better. I shouldn't have lied. I should have talked to you first. Please forgive me?

@_Shannyxo: I don't know, Ade. It's always one thing or another. You promised me nothing would change and every other day I feel us drifting apart.

@TripleAde: I know. I'm really sorry. It's just hard at school to make both groups work. But I have to do better.

@_Shannyxo: Sigh. If you say so.

@TripleAde: I do say so. And I say sorry again. I really am.

@_Shannyxo: Okay. Well, I've got to go and finish up some things. Chat later.

@TripleAde: What things?

@_Shannyxo: Just stuff.

@TripleAde: Ooh, what are you hiding? Tell me!

@_Shannyxo: I'm just doing stuff – stuff you don't care to ask me about most of the time. You only take an interest in my life when we're on here. The rest of the time you're embarrassed by me. I'll speak to you later, I guess. Bye.

@TripleAde: Okay. Bye.

Chapter 28
Shanice

Hey,

I feel like I'm at a crossroads in my friendship with Ade. I really don't know what to do. Gosh, I miss Mum. She would know what to do or what to say. I don't want to talk to Dad about it. He'll crack a joke, and it'll just make things worse. But, then again, how can anything get worse? I don't like writing when I'm upset, especially about my feelings.

Soz that I haven't shared anything remotely happy or interesting recently. I've just been trying to avoid Ade at all costs in school these days. I've been sitting by the door in lessons so I can make a dash for it when class is over. If you have any ideas on what to do, then I'm all ears!

I've been trying to take my mind off the situation by working on my memory scrapbook for Mum – it's shaping up to be quite the project. Remember when I said I'm not that creative? I actually am a little bit. I've come up with this really cool collage effect going right through the book. It's like I'm telling stories of Mum and her life with me in chronological order. However, it's taking me a long time to cut out all the pictures and arrange them in exactly the way I want.

I'm a little bit of a perfectionist. Everything has to be just right. I've had a sick idea to use old magazines to bring each section to life, and I'm using some of the text in them to make my own headlines for each page. Then I've drawn round the borders with my felt-tip pens, to bring it all together in a really colourful and vibrant way. By the time I'm done with this, I'll be able to go on one of those arts-and-crafts shows on TV.

Mrs P suggested that I interview my dad and James about when I was a baby. 'Life throws up many different challenges, experiences and unexpected events,' she said. 'Your book will have stories of your mum from your own perspective, but have you thought about your dad's and your brother's points of view? It can make for a rich and in-depth memory book.'

Hmm, how do you even do interviews? It just seems really hard. Do you just sit there, ask questions and see what they say? What if I don't like what they come out with? I don't want embarrassing stories in my book, thanks! It would be so James to say something about me farting and pooping myself as a baby.

This project has really lifted my mood and taken my mind off everything. I so want it to be special!

Chapter 29

Ade

Dear Diary,
SORRY I HAVEN'T WRITTEN IN YOU IN A
WHILE — BEING THE MOST POPULAR GIRL IN
SCHOOL IS TIME-CONSUMING. Okay, *one* of the
most popular girls — Aaliyah still gets a handful more
likes than I do on ChatBack, but I definitely still get
more than Amy, and everyone else at Archbishop
Academy.

It's crazy — I've not even been here a whole term,
but it feels like forever — in a good way. I'm not
trying to show off, but I've got more followers than
people who have been here since Year 7. I've even got
loads of random people from other schools following

me, liking my pictures and commenting under my photos with hearts and thumbs ups. The Triple As are kinda well known now for their viral dances and sick fashion sense — sometimes I wonder if we're the most popular girls at school, or the most popular girls in the whole town!

Everyone wants to be friends with the Triple As — well, except Shanice. She still claims I don't talk to her any more, but I don't think that's true — we spend hours talking on ChatBack! Well, usually getting into arguments about Amy and Aaliyah.

'I told you already,' she'll say sulkily. 'They are mean girls. They're horrible.'

She says I've changed, and maybe I have: I dress better, and I'm more confident. Aaliyah reckons Shanice is jealous of our friendship, and I'm starting to think that she's right. Sure, sometimes the girls can say things that are a bit below the belt, but they're only joking! They never mean it — and I made sure to tell Shanice that. And they wouldn't do it if they didn't know she'd rise to the bait. Every. Single. Time. She'll go off in a strop, shout something back at them when she could just ignore them altogether. She can be way too ~~boring~~ sensitive sometimes, and it's cramping my style.

Ugh, hang on. Mr Oppong can see me scribbling away during registration. I'll be back later to finish this off . . .

I'm back — and I am seriously upset. You know EVERYTHING I wrote earlier today? I have never been more wrong about anything ever. I'm so stupid. I was saying how Shanice is the issue, but now I think she might be the one who's actually right. Something happened today after school that I feel bad about. Okay, *really* bad about.

You know how Triple A are the sickest dancers in the area? Well, after weeks of basically being the best on every dance challenge on ChatBack, we decided to create our own. It's called the Pee-ew — you kinda hold your nose and wave your hand in front of your face while jumping on the spot. It looks a lot better than it sounds, trust me.

'Remind you of anyone?' Amy giggled as we practised after school in the park.

Aaliyah laughed really hard. 'The Smelly Shanice Powers!'

They collapsed into a fit of giggles.

'Don't be mean!' I said, but I have to admit I did giggle a bit too! I don't know how, but they have a way of making you laugh along with even the worst things they come out with.

Anyway, as usual, we used Aaliyah's tripod to record the dance, and it came out looking great. She added special effects, filters, the works, and said she'd upload it when she got in.

I didn't think much more of it. Then, just as I was getting ready for bed, my notifications on ChatBack started going crazy. I was excited at first – I knew the video would go viral! Aaliyah had so many comments and likes under her post I could barely keep up, but then I noticed how the video was captioned and couldn't believe my eyes.

Triple A presents THE SHANICE POWERS
CHALLENGE #nevershowerspowers
#shanicepowers #loner #loser

There we were, holding
our noses as we danced —
they'd made the dance about
Shanice! And it was going
viral.

   I was so shocked. I knew
they'd made a stupid joke about
her earlier, but this was completely
uncalled for. They'd gone too far. As
soon as I saw it, I messaged them to
take it down.

CHAPTER 30
∎
CHATBACK

@DoubleAmy: Don't be stupid! We have over a thousand likes and counting, and it's not even been up for long!

> @DoubleAaliyah: Yeah, Ade. Don't be such a baby.

@TripleAde: I'm not a baby. This isn't cool. It's cruel. At least change the name. Shanice doesn't deserve this – she hasn't done anything to you guys. She's my friend.

> @DoubleAaliyah: She's such a good friend that you didn't even invite her to your birthday party lol.

I felt a wave of shame as I read that, and didn't even reply because Aaliyah was right. I've been such a rubbish friend to Shanice. How did I let things get to this point? I'm still trying to pluck up the courage to message her, but I don't even know what to say. I've been a coward, and I'm still a coward :(

Chapter 31

Shanice

Hey,

This has got to be one of the hardest days ever. Like ever, ever. In the history of Shanice Powers.

It's so hard to even write this that I'm just gonna give you the highlights and go to bed. I'm so tired from crying all evening.

So I had to go to Dad's shop today after school. He wanted me to help him out with some packaging because he's still short-staffed. (How is that my problem? Talk about using me for free labour!!!) So I was still sulking because I'm yet to be given my bearded dragon (if she goes to another owner, I'll never forgive Dad).

Anyway, there I was, helping him against my will. He even made James come too. Dad is trying to launch his own hair-care products, and the manufacturer had got all the labels wrong, so James and I were helping Dad peel each label off and replace it with a brand-new one. Dad was looking so stressed out. They spelt our name wrong. Instead of Powers it says Powwer. Yikes.

Anyway, we were peeling and relabelling when James's phone started buzzing and buzzing. He looked at it and gave a big sigh, and then he looked at me and Dad before putting his phone away. I assumed it was his mates asking about his whereabouts. They can't live without each other, you see.

Buzz-buzz. It was going off again. By this point, Dad was giving him daggers.

James stood up and walked over to us.

'Dad, can Shanice and I have a break to get some food?' he said sheepishly.

Dad looked suspicious. I did too. James never bothers to include me in his getaways from the shop.

'Sure, but come straight back. We're on a roll, and we need to get these samples ready for tomorrow.'

He pulled a tenner from his pocket and put it in James's hand.

'Okay, we will,' James said, looking at me while nodding his head towards the door.

'Don't forget my change,' said Dad.

We left the shop and started walking towards Sandy's, the go-to local Caribbean place. So yummy. My belly started growling at the thought of the curry chicken, rice and peas and a large portion of plantain on the side – all washed down with pineapple juice.

As we walked, James suddenly turned to me.

'Yo, so this Ade girl – I thought you two were friends?'

I was confused. 'Yeah . . . we are . . . I mean . . . not as much as before but . . .'

'Well, she's not your friend,' he said.

He looked seriously uncomfortable as he shoved his phone in my face.

My heart sank. There were Ade, Amy and Aaliyah, on ChatBack, doing a stupid dance with a caption:

I felt sick. My whole world stopped. For what seemed like ages, we just stood in the middle of the pavement. My eyes started to fill up with tears and one dropped on to James's phone.

'Yeah, stay away from her and those girls. They're horrible.'

I couldn't say anything. I was completely lost for words. My throat was dry like a dusty desert.

By the time we'd got our food and were back at the shop, I had lost my appetite big time.

Why would Ade be so mean? I expected it from the other two . . . but it's like I'd never really known her at all. Had she been just like them all along? This was such a betrayal.

For the rest of the afternoon, I sat in silence in the shop – my sulking had turned to utter misery. My eyes were red from all the crying I was doing on my breaks in the bathroom.

On the way back home, Dad could tell I was close to crying again, but he didn't say anything. I think James must have told him what had happened when I'd been in the loo. He just looked really angry.

Everything is going from bad to worse to terrible. All I can think about are those hashtags – #nevershowerspowers #shanicepowers #loner #loser – playing in my head over and over again. I've gone viral. Yup, you heard it here first. I've gone viral on ChatBack. It's like some cruel, twisted joke, but it's not a joke . . . it's my life.

CHAPTER 32
CHATBACK

@TripleAde: Hey, Shanice, I hope you're okay. Just wanted to message about the post earlier today on ChatBack. I had no idea they were going to call the video that. I'm really, really sorry, Shanice :(I hope you believe me.

        @_Shannyxo: Lol, okay.

@TripleAde: I mean it. I didn't know. I really didn't.

        [@_Shannyxo is typing…]

@TripleAde: I'm so sorry.

[@_Shannyxo is typing…]

@TripleAde: What, Shanice?

[@_Shannyxo is typing…]

@_Shannyxo: Nothing.

@TripleAde: Nothing? It's not nothing though, is it?
Talk to me.

@_Shannyxo: I said nothing. Jeez.

@TripleAde: I'm trying to apologise to you. I'm really
sorry for what happened.

[@_Shannyxo is typing…]

@TripleAde: ???

[@_Shannyxo is typing…]

@TripleAde: Shanice?

@_Shannyxo: You've changed, I already told you. And I don't like who you've become. Ever since you started hanging around with Amy and Aaliyah, you barely even acknowledge me at school and you only talk to me on ChatBack. You didn't even invite me, your supposed best friend, to your birthday party. And, because I still wanted to be your friend, I've been putting up with it. But today crossed a line. More and more, I see you becoming a mean girl just like them. You guys deserve each other.

@TripleAde: Gosh. I'm really sorry, Shanice. I deserved that. I'll talk to them, I promise. I don't even want to be their mate after today. I swear I'll stand up to them.

@_Shannyxo: Don't even bother. I've told you millions of times how horrible they've been to me, and you've let it slide. You became part of their gang and just ignored me at school. You've never stood up for me. It's too late.

@TripleAde: I did stick up for you when I could! Of course I did! You know you're my best mate.

@_Shannyxo: No, I don't. You are not my best mate. You're not even my mate. You may not be a bully like they are, but you're just as bad. You're a coward, and I don't want anything to do with you, Ade. To think all this time I was upset at us drifting apart, but you know what? I'm better off without you. You don't deserve me as a friend. Goodbye.

@TripleAde: Shanice, wait. Can we talk about this properly? Off ChatBack? I'm really sorry, Shanice.

[You have been blocked by @_Shannyxo. You are no longer able to send or receive messages from this contact.]

Chapter 33
Shanice

Hey,

Ever since that tagged post, I've had so many people on
my ChatBack profile – urgh, I just wish I could disappear.
It's so embarrassing to go into school these days. It's
like everyone's laughing at me. Right, I'm going to delete
ChatBack. There's no reason why I should be on there at
all. Nothing good has come from it.

Oh, wait – Sophie AKA the most popular girl in Year 9
AKA my buddy has just followed me on ChatBack.

CHAPTER 34
■
CHATBACK

@Queen_Soph: Hey, you all right, babe?

@_Shannyxo: Hi!

(I've only really spoken to Ade on ChatBack. Sophie makes me nervous and shy – she's what people at Archbishop Academy call 'unreal'. It's pretty nice of her to message me, though . . .)

@Queen_Soph: What's new with you?

(What did she mean by that? She's probably seen me going viral – how tragic, I'm officially the most pathetic girl in school!)

@_Shannyxo: Nothing much, just doing homework.

@Queen_Soph: Urgh, I hardly did homework last year, it doesn't really count until you have exams.

@_Shannyxo: Oh really?

@Queen_Soph: Yeah, really, those teachers try to make everything about homework these days. It's never that deep.

@_Shannyxo: :)

@Queen_Soph: Anyway, so James Powers is your brother, right?

@_Shannyxo: Yeah, he is.

@Queen_Soph: I thought so! He's kinda unreal xx

@_Shannyxo: Is he?

@Queen_Soph: Yeah he is. There's just something about him, unreal and so cool too.

@_Shannyxo: Okay.

@Queen_Soph: Does he have a girlfriend?

@_Shannyxo: Not that I know of.

@Queen_Soph: Love to hear it! Do you mind putting in a good word for me?

@_Shannyxo: Good word?

@Queen_Soph: Yeah, like how helpful I've been as your buddy and all! Basically, just say I'm a nice girl.

@_Shannyxo: Okay.

@Queen_Soph: Thanks, babe! Imagine if I was his gf, we would be the most unreal couple at Archbishop <3

@_Shannyxo: :)

@Queen_Soph: Anyway, g2g, babe. Kisses xx

Just like that, she was gone again. Okay, this has confirmed it: I'm going to delete my ChatBack account. So much for it being nice of my oh-so-helpful buddy to message me. The last thing I need is to play matchmaker for Sophie.

Urgh, James unreal? Everything right now feels so surreal.

[*deletes ChatBack*]

To: <shanice.powers09@webmail.co.uk>
From: <oni.ade@webmail.co.uk>
Subject: Hey

I tried to message you on ChatBack and realised that you've blocked me. So I guess I'll have to email you instead.

I can't say I blame you for not wanting anything to do with me, but can we talk? I miss you. We're supposed to be best friends. Call me?

Ade

Chapter 35
Shanice

Hey,

Ade sent me an email today.

She really must be desperate. Running back because those girls have dropped her like a hot potato? Or maybe she now realises she has a mind of her own, and that friendship with them was always going to be a dead end. I'm still very hurt. I'm not going to reply. What's the point? We're not best friends any more. We're not even friends. It has been SO awkward at school. When I see her walking in my direction, I hide and don't make eye contact, but I know I can't avoid her forever . . . or can I? I'm getting pretty good at it.

I pretended I'd lost my voice in class today so I didn't have to speak when Mr Oppong asked me a question - I had to pull an 'I understand what you're saying but I can't reply' soz face. I don't think he believed me, but how could he check I was lying? :)

I'm just trying to be invisible to everyone at Archbishop, like a ghost.

BRB - Dad is calling me. I need to set the table for dinner.

You're not replying to my emails or phone calls, so am texting you. Shanice, I am so sorry for everything. Not just the other day – everything. I completely get if you never want to talk to me again, but I just want to be able to apologise to you for everything properly even if that's the case.

I'm so sorry :(Ade

Chapter 36
Shanice

Hey,

I'm back.

She just texted me. I forgot to block her on my phone. Urgh. Can't she just leave me alone? She needs to understand that she can't drop me and then pick me up whenever she wants. That's not how friendships work. All she had to do was be loyal. It was really that simple. Anyway, I don't need anybody to be my friend. Who needs them anyway? I'm so upset and still angry about the whole situation.

Chapter 37

Ade

Dear Diary,

TODAY HAS BEEN THE MOST HORRIBLE DAY
EVER. It's been three whole days since Shanice
blocked me on ChatBack, and she's still ignoring
my emails. She won't pick up my calls or reply to
my messages either. She doesn't even look at me at
school. It's like I'm a ghost. I've tried to approach her
a couple of times, but she never acknowledges me.
She just walks right past. I guess that's how she felt
when I wouldn't talk to her properly at school. I've
really messed things up.

Amy and Aaliyah, meanwhile, have gone right off
me because I want to patch things up with Shanice,

but I don't even care. I'm relieved, to be honest. Half the time I felt like a third wheel, a hanger-on. They think I didn't know that they would sneak off and hang out without me sometimes, and I'm sure they have secrets I don't know about. They were mean to everyone, all the time, and I guess, because I didn't want to be on the receiving end and I wanted to seem 'cool', I joined in or turned a blind eye. Even when it was to my best mate.

Now they give me the same dirty looks they gave Shanice, and even snicker when I walk past. I can't help but think how terrible I've been for not seeing just how horrible they are. And purely because it wasn't happening to me. I've already heard them calling me 'Aggy Ade' under their breath — thankfully, I binned their shoddy bracelet as soon as I saw that awful post. All this week I've been alone — something I put Shanice through because I thought I'd found better friends. I've never felt more guilty about anything ever.

Today, when I got back from school, I ran to my room and cried harder than I had all week. Aunty Kim's away in Crete with her friend from work, so I haven't been able to chat to her about it, and Bisi's way too loved up with her boyfriend so she's never here. Funmi is too young to understand. Mum has been working nights, so I haven't been able to talk to her — plus, I was kind of avoiding telling her. She was so upset when I didn't invite Shanice to my birthday, she probably even thinks I deserve this. Today she was supposed to be back on her regular rota though, and I desperately needed advice. After wiping my eyes, I went to find her in the living room. I could hear the TV, but when I got there it was *him*.

'Where's Mum?' I asked.

'She's at work. They needed her on the late shift again tonight.'

'Oh. Okay,' I said, crushed. I turned to leave, but he called after me. 'Your eyes are red. Everything okay?'

'Not really,' I said. I couldn't even be bothered to lie. 'Let me know when Mum's back, yeah?'

'Is there anything I can do to help?' he asked.

At that, I broke down. I was just too upset to do anything but cry about the mess I'd made.

'I've ruined everything,' I said, through wet, snotty sobs.

He tapped the sofa seat next to him. 'What happened?'

I sat down beside him. And then I told him everything — about ChatBack, about the Double As, about how rubbish a mate I'd been to Shanice, about my birthday, about the video. He sat and nodded thoughtfully throughout, like it was a super-important news segment.

'I feel awful,' I said, wiping my eyes. 'I'm a bad person.'

'You're not a bad person,' he said, passing me a tissue from his pocket. 'You're human. And we tend to make mistakes. All of us. Even the best ones. These mistakes can hurt people's feelings, but they can also be fixed.'

When I heard that, I felt even worse, thinking about how horrible I'd been to *him*. Here he was, trying to help, and I'd been such a brat ever since I'd met him.

'This is a mistake that you can and will fix,' he said. 'We just need to work out how.'

'I'm thinking of going round there or booking a hair appointment,' I said, wiping my eyes. 'But I'm scared she'll see it's me and refuse to come out.'

He thought for a moment, stroking his chin. 'Have you considered writing her a letter?'

'A letter?'

'Yes, a letter. When I was your age, people received more than just bills in the post.' He laughed. 'You said she'd blocked you on, what is it called? BackChat?'

'ChatBack,' I said. Normally, I would have rolled my eyes at that mistake, made fun of him in my head, but I didn't.

'Ah, ChatBack. Well, maybe you can write her a letter to really explain how sorry you are, and then she can decide if she wants to see you? Plus, you express yourself very well through writing, your mum says.'

I thought for a moment. 'That's a good idea,' I said, sniffing.

Sure, letters are a bit old school — they make me think of *Jane Eyre* — but that's not necessarily a bad thing, since ChatBack partly got me into this mess in the first place. I needed to do something. It was my last chance.

'I'm going to do that right now. This means a lot. Thanks, Emmanuel,' I said, probably using his name for the first time in my life.

He smiled widely. 'You are very welcome, Ade. Any time. And good luck.'

Can you believe it? Emmanuel was actually there for me in my hour of need when no one else was around. I think he might be all right after all.

Yet another thing I was wrong about; I really am so stupid. Such an idiot!

Anyway, this idiot wrote the letter to Shanice, and I was as honest and real as I could be. I took the bus to her house and posted it this afternoon. The envelope got damp from the sweat on my hands — I was *that* nervous. I really hope this works . . . I don't know what I'll do if it doesn't.

Chapter 38
Shanice

HEY!

GUESS WHAT? GOOD NEWS AT LONG LAST!

You're probably wondering what it could be. I'll give you one guess.

Hmm, maybe two guesses. But, if you know me by now, you'll only need one.

Bearded dragon :)

Yes, she's mine. Can you believe it? Dad surprised me this morning with her. I had just got back from swimming with James, and I walked through the door, and there she was on the table. At first, I thought this was some kind of joke, or that I was dreaming, but there she was in her glass tank looking just so beautiful and green.

'What's going on here?' I said to James.

'Dunno. How would I know?' he said with a puzzled expression on his face.

Dad was nowhere to be seen! Then, as I was taking her out of her tank, he walked in and said: 'I see you've met again – hope you like her!'

'I *love* her, Dad – thank you, thank you!!' I said.

He looked so pleased with himself. I know I give Dad a hard time these days, but he is doing his best. It can't be easy for him managing everything, but he really does come through for me every time. I'm going to try and show him how grateful I am / go easier on him from now on.

Did you know that bearded dragons get their name from the spiny projections under their chins that resemble a man's beard? When they feel threatened or excited, they puff out their beards and open their mouths to make themselves look bigger. Awesome, right?

What should I call her? I'm thinking something cool and snazzy like a nickname rather than a boring first name. I'll keep you posted.

I'm super happy. I'm going to look after her so well. I have such a lot to learn about her too. Having a pet full time is a big responsibility – that's one of the things Ms Davies always lectures her customers about.

Well, I'm going to be the most responsible thirteen-year-old pet-owner ever.

42 Welton Road
Rainham
Essex
RM13 8QP

Dear Shanice,

I've tried messaging on ChatBack, texting, sending you emails, and this feels like the last resort: a letter. I feel like a right stalker, to be honest — the last letter I wrote was to Father Christmas when I was six — but I'll give it a go.

It's not ideal, contacting you like this, but I'm hoping it will help me be a little more honest, with you and with myself. It's a bit like writing in my diary — Aunty Kim always has a go at me for being on my phone too much when I could be writing. I always reply that texting counts as writing, even though I am doing it on my phone. But she argues that it isn't the same, and now I think she has a point. Writing this down properly is really making me feel I can get everything off my chest once and for all.

Firstly, I want to apologise to you. I do get why you don't want to talk to me, and why you might never want to again. I haven't been a good friend to you, let alone a best friend, though I think that was partly because I wasn't really being myself. I honestly had no idea that Amy and Aaliyah were going to write that horrible caption on the video – I swear. As soon as I saw it, I knew the Triple As were done for good. But still – it should never have got that far. And that was down to me.

If only I'd spoken up for you sooner, cared less about what people thought. You warned me so many times about how mean they were, and the truth is I did hear you, but I just didn't listen. Maybe, because they were being nice to me, I felt safer being part of their 'gang' than being outside it.

You made me feel so welcome when I first came to Archbishop Academy, like a real friend does. Instead of returning the favour, I threw it back in your face. I left you out. I ignored you. And what for? A few extra likes on ChatBack? I ended up hurting a person I really care about, all to pretend to be someone I'm not, for people who didn't really care anyway.

I told myself everything was okay because we were still friends online, but that's not real life, is it? And the stuff we spoke about, the secrets we shared, the laughs we had — everything we shared offline was so much more real. Throughout our friendship, you liked me for who I am and tried to make me stay true to myself, but I think I was just desperate to fit in. You're right — I am a coward. You have always just been yourself, and that takes real courage. I see that now — I only wish I had earlier. It may be too late, but I'm writing this in the hope that it isn't.

Since I'm trying to be completely honest, if I were in your position, I'd probably never talk to me again. I'd probably read this sweat-stained letter (sorry — I was nervous), crumple it up, throw it in the fireplace and forget all about it. I wouldn't give me the time of day. But you're not me — and that's what makes you so special. You are your own person. You think for yourself, and you call things as you see them, like you did with the Double As. As I've said, I completely understand if you don't want to be friends any more. But I do want you to know that I mean every word of this letter and hope you can forgive me.

Thanks for reading,

Ade x

Chapter 39

Shanice

Hey,

Just writing after breakfast because I've got a busy day ahead – so this will be the only time I have to update you, and what an update it is! I'm spending the day at the salon, but before that I'm going to the arts-and-crafts store to pick up a few bits for my memory book. It's coming along so well – it's going to take me a little longer than I'd planned, but I'm in no rush. I would rather it be perfect. **I think Mum would be so proud – even James seemed impressed at breakfast this morning.**

'Wow, this looks so sick. I didn't realise you were that creative,' he said, surprised.

'I know, right? Neither did I!' I smiled back.

But he couldn't help but give me some unsolicited advice!

'However, If I were you, I would sketch round the stickers and colour in that bit instead,' he said, pointing to the page I had turned to.

'No thanks. I know what I'm doing,' I said, moving the book away from him.

Gosh, he really thinks he knows everything, but this is my special project. I'll do it the way I want to, thank you very much.

I couldn't help but feel proud of myself. I would have loved to show it to Ade. She would be so into it, especially because I've used as much pink as possible everywhere. Between my bearded dragon and working on my memory book, I haven't really had a chance to think about her or the stuff that's been going on. I'm back to keeping myself to myself in school, and it's like I never met Ade.

Mrs P has noticed we're not friends any more too. She pulled me aside at lunchtime.

'Is everything okay, Shanice? I've noticed you and Ade don't seem to be hanging out like you used to.'

I told her what had happened on ChatBack, and how Ade had stopped being a good friend to me.

'I understand how hurt you are. You must be so disappointed in her – you were inseparable at one point.'

'Yeah, we were, but she chose those girls over me, and now I'm a laughing stock at school.'

'You're not a laughing stock. You kids have the memory of a goldfish – everyone will have forgotten this ChatBack business by tomorrow,' she said.

'Well, I'll remember it forever. It was so embarrassing,' I whispered.

'You have every right to be upset, but remember you had a special bond. Maybe one day Ade will come to miss your friendship, and regret getting involved with those silly girls. You know, best friends sometimes go through difficult times, but I believe a true friendship like yours can survive a few knocks along the way.'

'I seriously doubt that, Mrs P. Dad says I'm being stubborn, but I have to be. She hurt me really badly – am I now just expected to forgive her?' I said, annoyed.

'Nobody expects you to do anything, Shanice, but I know you miss her,' she said with a hopeful smile on her face, as she walked off to her next class.

Yes, I do miss her . . . often. That's the thing. Our friendship was fun, and she was like a sister to me. Maybe I should have replied to her last text message? Maybe she really is sorry? Well, it's too late now. It's done. I'm sure she'll find herself another best friend at Archbishop.

I was staring at a picture of Mum when James walked in with the day's post.

'When did you start receiving mail? Urgh, it's a bit soggy,' he said, handing a letter to me.

I knew that handwriting immediately. It was Ade's. My heart started beating really fast. Why is she sending me letters? I didn't want to open it while James was still in the kitchen, but as soon as he'd left the room I ripped it open and started reading.

WOW.

Ade has written me a letter apologising for everything. I think she really means it. It must have taken guts to write this and then deliver it right to my home. I am still hurt, but I do miss her. She's not a bad person. We all make mistakes . . . doesn't mean we have to be punished forever, does it? That would be a bit extreme . . .

I looked at that picture of Mum. What would she do? She would definitely say I should forgive. I know she would have loved Ade.

Okay, deep breath . . .

CHAPTER 40

CHATBACK

[*logs into ChatBack – unblocks Ade*]

@_Shannyxo: Hi, Ade.

                        @Ade4everx: OMG, Shanice, hi!!

[@_Shannyxo is typing…]

            @Ade4everx: I'm so, so, so sorry for everything, please
                               forgive me. I've missed you so much.

[@_Shannyxo is typing…]

@_Shannyxo: I've missed you too.

Chapter 41

Ade

Dear Diary,

SORRY FOR BEING A BIT AWOL RECENTLY; THERE'S BEEN LOADS FOR ME AND SHANICE TO CATCH UP ON, AND THERE'S LOADS FOR ME TO CATCH YOU UP ON TOO!

Funmi finally lost the last of her baby teeth. But, instead of being a normal person and putting it under her pillow for money from the tooth fairy (who she still doesn't realise is Mum), she's been walking around with it in her pocket and grossing me out by shoving it in my face at breakfast. She's something else.

Bisi is . . . well, Bisi. She's still a moody so-and-so, but I think this boyfriend of hers might actually be doing something right, since she's actually not biting everyone's head off every hour of the day! (It's only every other hour now.)

Aunty Kim still comes down as much as she can, and, when she does, makes appointments at Powers so she can 'bump into' Shanice's dad, Matthew . . . Yuck.

Anyway, everything's kinda been the same except, guess what? Me and Shanice met up the other week at Powers.

It was right after I sent her that cringey (but totally necessary) letter. I almost didn't go. Can you believe it? Even though I was desperate to sort things out, I was scared too. I haven't been that emotionally honest with anyone, other than you and Aunty Kim (she can get anything out of me — that woman should work for the FBI!), so I was really nervous when I got Shanice's message on ChatBack saying that she missed me too.

I wasn't at all sure what to expect, but I thought I'd try my luck and ask her if we could meet up at her dad's shop. She said to come the next day at lunchtime, and I was really excited at first, but then I realised I couldn't be sure whether Shanice had forgiven me or not, so I was a bag of nerves, worrying whether I should even bother. I started imagining what might happen when I got there. What if she just wanted to have a go at me? Or get me back with some sort of revenge plot to embarrass me? I mean, that would be a very Double-A move, and she's nothing like them, but thoughts like that were buzzing around in my head.

I ended up talking to *him* — sorry, Emmanuel (old habits die hard) — of all people. He's the one who convinced me to go, gave me a lift there and all. Said good mates are hard to come by, and that she was probably dying to see me too, or she wouldn't have agreed to it.

As it turns out, Emmanuel and I actually have quite a lot in common — he has pretty good taste in music and is addicted to salt-and-vinegar crisps as well! Since he gives me lifts everywhere all the time, he can't be that bad. Plus, he makes Mum happy, which counts for something. I like seeing her happy, even though I catch her doing this annoying smug smile whenever she sees us sharing a joke or getting on. Ugh.

Anyway, when he dropped me off at Powers,

the first person I saw was Shanice's dad. I'd been so worried about bumping into him; I was sure he'd be fuming at me. But instead he looked relieved to see me and gave me a massive smile.

'Ade! How nice to see you,' he said, hands on his hips. He nodded at the brown leather couch. 'Someone's waiting to see you.'

And there was Shanice, sitting in the very same spot where I'd first met her, journal at her side and her nose in a dog-eared old beauty magazine. I tapped her on the shoulder and wondered what her expression would be when she saw me. Thankfully, she smiled.

'Hey,' she said, putting down the magazine.

I shuffled awkwardly and looked down at the floor. 'Hey.'

We didn't say anything for a bit. We both just kind of laughed nervously at each other. I started to panic that things might not ever be the same again. What if it was too late? What if she could forgive me, but couldn't forget? I started to apologise again.

'I just wanted to say that I'm so—'

'Ade, I know,' she said. 'I unblocked you on

ChatBack for a reason. I accept your apology, okay?' She laughed again. 'You really do love repeating yourself, don't you?'

I laughed too, this time without the nerves. 'Oi! So what if I do? Better safe than sorry!' I said with a giggle. Shanice started giggling too, and suddenly we were hugging. It had been so long — too long!

'Hey, I saw your new screen name,' she said once we'd calmed down. 'Ade4everx. I like it.'

'Me too,' I said with a grin. 'It just feels right. Not someone I'm pretending to be, or someone I was once upon a time, but just . . . me. You know?'

'I know,' she said.

And that's why I've been AWOL, you see. You'll be glad to know it's only because Shanice and I have been hanging out a lot recently. To make up for being a rubbish mate, I gave her journal a wicked makeover, used all my nicest stickers that I'd been saving to cover my English folder with and everything. She said I didn't have to, but also that she loved it!

We're back to being as thick as thieves, much to Mr Oppong's annoyance, as he can never shut us up during tutor time. He lets us off though, because I know I'm definitely his favourite pupil in 8O. Shanice still isn't a fan, and I still don't know what she sees in Mrs P. But that's what's great about our relationship — even though we're different, we can see things from each other's perspective. She's gone from thinking Mr Oppong is the worst to thinking he's 'meh', and I've gone from thinking Mrs P is a bore to thinking she's okay. I guess that's something . . .

As for the Double As, it's weird to think we were ever friends. The way they treat people at school is so mean. I honestly have no idea how I convinced myself it was okay, just because they weren't doing it to me. They don't talk to me at all now. They look right through me, but they do the same to Shanice too, which is actually an improvement from before. In fact, they did speak to me just once, to ask me to give back my bracelet. I did it with glee.

Ade and I got matching silver necklaces the next day. Her side of the heart says 'Best' and mine says 'Friend', and when you put them next to each other it spells the word out in full and makes a whole heart. It's a bit soppy, but you know how I love my jewellery.

Double A are still the coolest girls in school. Their dances go viral every other week. They have loads of followers, even more now, and get the most likes on their pictures — and I couldn't care less. Why? Well, because I have the most important likes of all. My family (annoying as they are) like me. Shanice, my best friend, likes me. And I like me. And there's no amount of likes online I'd swap for the life I have offline.

Speaking of online, just got a ChatBack notification from Shanice. I think she has some questions about English. Will speak to you (well, write in you) later.

Till then,

out x

Chapter 42
Shanice

Hey!

I can't speak for long as I have English homework that's really causing me the biggest frown lines ever, urghhhh. I usually love English, but I'm not loving this new assignment at all. And it's due tomorrow so I need to get on with it before my frown lines multiply!

Anyway, on to happier things . . . I've had the . . . THE best few days with Ade. For the first time in ages, I feel happy. For such a long time, I couldn't even remember what this feeling felt like . . . It reminds me of when Mum was around, and life just felt . . . you know . . . normal.

Dad, me and James had a bit of a moment when I showed them my finished memory book.

'Shanice, it's beautiful!' I could see Dad's face light up as I turned to a new page.

Then there was that picture of us as a family, from Mum's last Christmas, and, as he took my hand, his eyes started to get all heavy and watery. James being James made a joke about our silly paper hats, and we all laughed. And then James actually said Mum would have been proud of me.

My memory book is now hidden in a special place in the house. I've told James and Dad they can have a look at it whenever they want. I do really love my little family – James still annoys me though. I can't wait till he goes to uni and I can have his room. He has his own little bathroom that I've always been jel of.

I've been spending time with Ade in and out of school, which I've loved. She's truly the funniest and the best friend in the entire world. Last week, we went to the arcade with Aunty Kim – we laughed so much I almost threw up. It was that funny. I'd just had a burger, cheesy loaded fries, a large glass of Fanta (with no ice ofc), and then Ade started making the funniest faces, using her straws and doing an impression of one of our teachers – I couldn't help but screech with laughter.

Anyway, Aunty Kim is spending a lot of time at my dad's shop these days. She comes in for a hair appointment and then just lingers and lingers and lingers . . . In my head, I'm like, *Go home!* She makes Dad laugh though, which is good to see!

Ade seems to think this is all part of Aunty Kim's master plan to become my stepmum . . . Don't get me wrong, Aunty Kim is lovely, but I'm not looking for a new mum – and Dad is not looking for a new wife! – so I'm keeping an eye on her :) She is great though – always looking out for me and getting me presents. Well, I'll accept the presents for now . . . and the outings. She's taking us bowling next week. I am so good at it (Ade not so much hehehe).

Right, I need to do this homework, then get ready for bed. So much has happened this year, both good and bad stuff. I don't expect things to be perfect all the time – life always has its ups and downs – but right now all is good with the world and my little life bubble.

Anyway,

G2G x

Shajida

Shajida

Khatun

Shajida